A CANDLELIGHT ECSTASY ROMANCE

"You're so sure of yourself," she cried, *"Do you always get what you want, Cord Harding?"*

"If I want it badly enough," he told her without hesitation, the certainty in his words a weapon itself. "And I do want you, Savannah Emery."

His hand dropped caressingly down the length of her side, the fingers sliding possessively over her breast. He groaned, a husky sound of male desire, and Savannah felt the extent of her own reaction. A part of her was stirring, responding to Cord's implicit demands. She trembled.

"You won't be sorry, sweetheart," he murmured.

Dear Reader:

In response to your enthusiasm for Candlelight Ecstasy Romances, we are now increasing the number of titles per month from two to three.

We are pleased to offer you sensuous novels set in America depicting modern American women and men as they confront the provocative problems of a modern relationship.

Throughout the history of the Candlelight line, Dell has tried to maintain a high standard of excellence, to give you the finest in reading pleasure. It is now and will remain our most ardent ambition.

Vivian Stephens
Editor
Candlelight Romances

WAGERED WEEKEND

Jayne Castle

A CANDLELIGHT ECSTASY ROMANCE

Published by
Dell Publishing Co., Inc.
1 Dag Hammarskjold Plaza
New York, New York 10017

Dell ® TM 681510, Dell Publishing Co., Inc.

ISBN: 0-440-19413-X

Printed in the United States of America

First printing—July 1981

CHAPTER ONE

Savannah Emery was aware of him the moment he entered the room. Everyone was. It wasn't just his sheer size, although Cordell Harding's six feet four inches of lean height and massive shoulders made him easy to spot in the crowd. Nor was it the surprisingly thick, uncompromising red of his hair. It was the fact that he was the boss and everyone at Mel North's party that night worked for him, including Savannah. She heard the ripple of polite greetings and office banter and realized with sure instinct that Cord Harding was making his way across the room in her direction.

With a casual deliberation she gave the cards in her hands one more shuffle, tilted her neat head of sleekly knotted seal-brown hair, and flashed her familiar, laughing smile at the others around the table. In the dim lighting Mel had arranged for the room few people seemed to notice that tonight the smile didn't reach the tawny gold eyes. Those who knew it didn't were far too sympathetically polite to say anything.

"If you'll excuse me," she said lightly to the other card players, "I'm going to take a break. Go on without me." Out of the corner of her eye she could see that Harding was clearly en route to the card table. She wanted out of there and fast.

"You can't quit now, Savannah," George Streeter protested with a theatrically pained expression on his boyish face. "You've won nearly all the chips!" A chorus of laughing agreement and pleas to continue ensued.

"But I always thought the best time to quit was when one was ahead," Savannah remarked innocently, rising gracefully to her feet. Her tall, elegantly proportioned figure moved with unconsciously smooth coordination. If someone had commented on her grace, she would have laughed ruefully and explained that anyone standing a bare inch under six feet and built like an amazon had to develop some compensating characteristics.

"You have to give us a chance to recoup our fortunes," someone groaned, indicating the huge pile of chips stacked in front of Savannah's seat.

Savannah's smile widened, and leaning forward, she pushed the chips into an untidy pile in the middle of the table. "As none of us high rollers has backed up any of these chips with so much as a penny, I can afford to be generous and surrender the entire pot!"

"Oh, well," George chuckled, beginning to dole

out the plastic markers to the others, "I suppose it might be fun for someone else to get a chance at winning. I must say, your luck has been phenomenal tonight, Savannah. If it keeps up, you ought to try Vegas."

"You know what they say," piped up another, a slightly drunken female, from the other side of the table. "Unlucky in love . . ."

There was an instant of embarrassed silence as first the speaker and then the other card players realized just what had been said. Savannah felt the discomfort of the small group and deliberately forced a light laugh.

"Lucky in cards," she retorted, finishing the trite cliché. "Go ahead and tell yourselves that, if it makes you feel any better. I'm sticking by my story that any luck I've had tonight is the result of superior skill and mental ability!"

There was general laughter as the players relaxed, and Savannah took advantage of it to make her exit. She slipped through the crowd of her co-workers who were arranged in various standing and sitting positions around the room, heading toward the bar Mel had set up in the corner. Somewhere in the gathering Jeff Painter and Alison Sayer, the couple whose engagement had provided Mel with the excuse to throw one of his famous parties, were standing close together, chatting with the others. Savannah resisted the impulse to seek them out yet again with her angry, bitter gaze. *You can't lose what you never really had,* she lectured herself for the hundredth time and tried to ignore the other argument: that

9

she'd come very close to having Jeff Painter for her own. If she'd only had a bit more time. . . . But time was something that had been denied her, thanks to the arbitrary business decisions of Cord Harding. It wasn't quite fair to blame her boss for Jeff's unexpected transfer down the coast to San Diego last month, but in her present resentful mood, Savannah was willing to do it.

The bar was a serve-yourself affair stocked with a wide variety of beverages and liquors. Mel loved throwing parties and always did it first class: Savannah poured herself another glass of the California zinfandel she had been drinking, dutifully reminded her usually aggressive common sense that she hadn't yet eaten dinner and really ought to be careful, and then downed a healthy swallow. This would be her last glass, she decided firmly. Still, it would be better to be remembered for having gotten slightly tipsy at this party than for having burst into angry tears or made a scene.

"I understand you left the card table as the undisputed winner of the evening," said a deep, richly masculine voice behind her.

Savannah turned in surprise, the warm gold eyes narrowing in deliberation, to face the last person she wanted to talk to tonight. Up close Cord Harding's ruggedly carved features were dominated by a pair of ruthlessly perceptive gray-green eyes. Arrogantly high cheekbones, a forceful chin, and lines that reflected his thirty-seven years of hard work and driving will fit together in a face that no one in his right mind would call handsome. Handsome implied a superficiality that was totally lacking in this man. And the very feral smile to which she was now being treated did little to soften the blatant maleness of him.

"The term 'winner' can be relative," she told him in a carefully polite, off-putting way, her gaze going past one of his broad shoulders to scan the room in an idle fashion. At twenty-eight, Savannah had developed a casually regal personality that went well with her face and figure. She could be *very* off-putting when she chose. The contours of her face were feminine but not soft. People didn't make the mistake of calling her beautiful, but striking was a word that many found applicable. And when she smiled, charming was a description that came to most people's minds. It was the smile that could so easily negate the haughty effect.

"I disagree," Cord said smoothly, shifting just slightly, enough to interrupt her view of the room full of co-workers dressed in the easygoing West Coast style. "A winner is someone who gets what he sets out to get. It's that simple."

"You should know, Mr. Harding," she retorted with mocking demureness, meeting his eyes over the rim of her glass. "You generally seem to get what you want. You've done very well for yourself what with owning your own engineering firm and making a success out of it before you've even turned forty." Very well, she added silently, remembering the gossip that said he was a classic self-made man who had started working in construction before he was out of high school. He'd gone to night school to get an

11

engineering degree and a background in business. After that there had been no stopping him. Less than two months ago he'd moved his headquarters from the San Diego office of his firm to the one in Costa Mesa where Savannah worked. It was the first time she'd met him. Her work in the personnel department had pitched her into two or three minor confrontations with him to date, confrontations she'd won when he had finally acknowledged her professional ability.

"Thank you," he murmured silkily, the gray-green eyes probing her features. She knew what he was looking for and she refused to give him the satisfaction of finding it. It was the same thing other people in the room had sought to know and Savannah wished the firm were a lot larger and more impersonal. No one, she told herself violently, was going to know how angry and hurt she was.

"The only problem with receiving a compliment from you is that one can't be quite sure whether it's genuine or merely some of the superficial, polite patter you've picked up in your career as a personnel officer," Cord went on consideringly, reaching for a glass and pouring himself a splash of something clear and potent.

Savannah let one dark brow rise aloofly. "You amaze me," she said dryly, watching as he set down the bottle he had just wielded and leaned his large frame against the padded bar. In spite of Savannah's height, Cord was several inches taller than she and there was something mildly unsettling about having him quite so close. Instinctively she wanted to move

12

away, but she had far too much pride to allow a trace of her unease to show. "I would have thought that with your unerring instinct for business and people you would have learned to sort out the truth."

"My, this conversation is turning personal in a hurry, isn't it?" he remarked interestedly, greenish eyes gleaming.

"Not through any fault of mine," Savannah informed him loftily, glancing away to hide a tinge of pink she felt flowing gently into her cheeks.

"I don't mind," he told her softly, and she could feel him watching her profile.

"My years of experience in the personnel line tell me it's highly unwise for the boss to have personal discussions with employees," she informed him with an attempt at lightness. Unfortunately, in her effort not to look at him, her eyes had, of their own accord, automatically sought out Jeff and Alison across the room. The sight did nothing for her mood. Jeff's dark head was bent intimately over the delicate, blond Alison in a protective way that made Savannah wince inwardly. Jeff had never adopted quite that attitude toward herself but, then, it was probably easy for a man to feel protective toward someone small and dainty like Alison. . . .

"And my years of experience as a man tell me a personal discussion is the best way to lead up to an invitation for dinner," he drawled.

Savannah's head snapped around as she frowned up at him. "I've told you on two occasions that I'm not interested, Mr. Harding," she reminded him bluntly.

"Let me see," he said slowly, thoughtfully. "On the first occasion you had just finished chewing me out for failing to pay proper attention to the employees' club. I asked you if you wanted to continue the discussion over dinner and you nearly took my head off."

"I already had a dinner engagement that evening," she reminded him stiffly, remembering that she had taken his invitation as a sign he was not treating the personnel issue at hand very seriously.

"So I discovered. With the gallant Mr. Painter. A couple of weeks after that Mr. Painter was transferred to San Diego—"

"*You* had him transferred!" Savannah couldn't resist saying pointedly and immediately could have bitten out her tongue.

"I'm a businessman, Savannah," Cord growled repressively. "You surely don't believe I've gotten where I am by making decisions like transferring a man simply because he's dating a woman I want to take out to dinner?"

"Of course not!" she agreed, her fingers tightening around the glass in her hand as she experienced a wave of embarrassment. It was true. A man such as Cord Harding would keep the business and personal sides of his life separate. One didn't become successful by combining them. "I didn't mean to imply you had done it for—for personal reasons." But the end result was the same, she added silently, and Cord knew it. Everyone in the room knew it by now.

"He wouldn't have been any good for you, Savannah," Cord suddenly stated in that deep, gravelly voice that always managed to make a listener pay attention. His attitude was so clearly that of a more worldly-wise man attempting to advise an overly emotional female that she wanted to scream.

"I don't intend to discuss my private life with you, Mr. Harding."

"I can see that," he murmured. "If I agree not to bring up the subject of Jeff Painter again this evening, will you have dinner with me?"

"I'm really not in a terrific mood tonight. I'd be lousy company," Savannah said briefly.

"I'll take my chances."

Savannah, rapidly losing her patience, met his eyes with a coolness she was far from feeling and saw in the green depths exactly what she had suspected. Cord Harding was testing the ground, trying to ascertain if, having lost one man, she was looking for another with which to salvage her pride. In a typically male manner he was willing to take advantage of the situation, and the knowledge infuriated her. Men! Right now she could cheerfully do without the lot of them! Did this arrogant creature really believe she was so dumb as to think he was bowled over by her startling beauty and sex appeal? Harding must have decided that, in an emotionally weakened condition, Savannah Emery would be easy prey.

"One more time, Mr. Harding. No. Thank you." She smiled as she said the words, but it wasn't her real smile and he must have known it.

Harding took a deep breath and a swallow of his drink, his eyes never leaving hers. She could see his expression hardening with a measure of determination and wanted to laugh aloud. How frustrating it must be for him to have a woman be so damn difficult! Not at all what he was probably accustomed to in the opposite sex. Somehow she felt a little better. As if she had repaid him in a small way for the hurt and humiliation he had inflicted on her with a simple, everyday business decision.

"I think you ought to accept my invitation," Cord said finally, and she could sense him willing her to do so.

"Why?" she taunted. "I'm not starving."

"Everyone here tonight knows about your crush on Jeff," he began softly.

"My crush!" she breathed, incensed. "I'm not an adolescent who doesn't understand her own emotions!"

"No," he agreed at once. "You're a woman who deserves something better than what Painter could have given you!"

"And you, I suppose, could give it to me?" she challenged, trying to leash her temper.

"If I were foolish enough to answer that, I'd never get you out to dinner." He suddenly chuckled. "And I want you to come. For your own sake as much as anything else."

"What great benefit will I derive except a free meal that you'll probably write off on your taxes?" she demanded, growing increasingly angry.

"You will have the very human pleasure of showing everyone here, including Jeff, that you're not exactly carrying a torch," he responded at once.

"Meaning there's nothing quite as dramatic as

leaving on the arm of one man to demonstrate to another that he wasn't all that important?" she hazarded. One sandaled foot tapped the floor gently beneath the hem of her sleek, summer dress of emerald green.

"Precisely." He waited expectantly.

"Why should you want to do me such a favor?" Savannah drawled, eyeing him speculatively. She knew very well why he was doing it. Mr. Cordell Harding was on the make tonight and she was the chosen victim because he thought she would be the most vulnerable.

"Let's just say I'm interested in furthering the cause of employer-employee relations," he said smoothly, the corner of his hard mouth crooking slightly as he apparently saw victory in sight.

"I'm sure you mean well, Mr. Harding, but the answer is still no. I'll summon the courage to walk out of here alone. It will be very character building, I'm sure." She grinned baitingly, wondering how long he would persist before going in search of another companion for the evening. Would he seek out another lone female in the crowd? It wasn't like Harding to try and date his employees. In fact she didn't know of a single instance so far, other than herself. Why was she the lucky lady?

"You're being too hasty, Savannah. Just think of how much frustration you could work off by spending an entire evening yelling at me for having transferred Jeff at such an inopportune time."

He had a point there, although she was loath to admit it. There would be a certain satisfaction in

17

getting even with this man who had so upset her plans. Perhaps the decision to disrupt her life had been made for purely business reasons, but the least he could do now was be sorry about it. Which he obviously was not.

"That would be childish of me, wouldn't it?" she returned haughtily.

"Very." He laughed abruptly. "But I'm prepared to be understanding."

"The answer is still no." Savannah took a sip of her wine, barely noticing that the level of the glass had gone down considerably.

"So adamant," he approved mockingly. "Tell me, would you like to take out your vengeance on me in a less personal way?"

"Now what are you suggesting?" she asked with a touch of hostility.

"I'll play some cards with you. If your luck is as good as your other opponents say it is, you'll be able to demolish me. Wouldn't that be pleasant?"

Savannah stared at him wordlessly, trying to sort out his strategy. Why should he want to gamble with her? On the other hand, there was something intriguing about the idea of defeating him, even at something as unimportant as a game of cards.

"We were playing blackjack earlier," she mused thoughtfully. "Not a lot of skill involved, just luck. . . ."

"Suits me." He smiled and she wondered if he knew how sharklike his smile could be. There was a challenging gleam in his eyes, a waiting look on the hard features of his face. Suddenly the urge to get

18

back at him in some more tangible way than simply refusing a dinner invitation was riding Savannah.

"All right," she said a trifle recklessly. "If that's what you want. . . ."

"I'll get us some cards and chips," he offered.

"What? We're not playing for real money?" she mocked.

"I'm prepared to be defeated by you but not financially ruined," he joked.

Savannah was aware a few minutes later that everyone knew a card game with the boss was under way in a quiet corner of the room but no one tried to invite himself into the game. As if sensing that the match was a private one, the others steered clear, giving Savannah and Cord a certain amount of privacy. The noise and laughter of the crowd provided a shield that kept their conversation from being overheard. Silently Savannah dealt the first hand.

"George and the rest were right." Cord grinned ruefully sometime later as he pushed another pile of chips across the table to add to Savannah's growing stack. "You are on a winning streak tonight. Care to switch to gin rummy for a while? I might have a better chance at that!"

Savannah, who had been playing with silent, deadly concentration glanced up briefly and shrugged. "Whatever you like. You'll be out of chips in a few more plays anyway," she said with satisfaction.

"I have the feeling that with very little effort you could be extremely rough on a man's ego," Cord noted, watching her deal the gin hand.

"Care to quit?" She smiled with anticipation, the

golden eyes gleaming at him. He had been right, she decided. It had been satisfying to trounce him so easily.

"Oh, no. Pride demands I stick it out to the bitter end," he sighed, picking up the cards.

Savannah's luck held through a round of gin rummy. She really couldn't lose tonight, she thought almost gleefully. The wine and the pleasure of a truly massive victory were going to her head and she knew it, but she had no wish to stop now. Not until she cleaned Cord Harding out.

"Well," he groaned finally, carefully counting his remaining chips. "I can think of only one way to make this game last more than another hand."

"What's that?" she demanded, preparing to deal once more.

"I'll have to start winning," he murmured.

"You," she announced with unkind cheerfulness, "haven't got a chance. You can see for yourself that I can't lose. Not tonight. Why don't you just throw in the towel and admit I've beaten you?"

"You'd like that?" he inquired curiously, propping his elbow on the table and resting his chin on one large hand.

"It was the whole point of the game, wasn't it?" she retorted. "To give me a way to work off my childish aggressions?" A subtle pleasure curved her lips. "Why drag out the inevitable? How about betting all or nothing?"

"That would get matters over with in a hurry, wouldn't it?" he responded almost carelessly. "Okay, all or nothing it is."

After an exhilarating series of wins, the outcome of the decisive play was a distinct shock to Savannah. She lost.

"No!" she yelped, impulsively putting a protective hand over her chips as Cord reached for them.

"You're not going to turn out to be a poor loser, are you?" he asked blandly, his hand hovering over her treasure. There was laughter in the cloudy-sea eyes. Arrogant male laughter that made Savannah more annoyed than she already was over the loss.

"Let's go back to blackjack," she insisted. "Just one hand."

"What have you got to bet?" he demanded reasonably enough, withdrawing his fingers from the vicinity of her chips.

"Your dinner invitation," she offered, inspiration striking. "I'll have dinner with you if you win this round." She couldn't bear to walk away from the table now and leave him the victor.

"Well . . ." he hesitated briefly, and Savannah rushed to prod him into agreeing.

"Unless you're afraid your new luck won't hold," she chided.

"I can take a dare as well as the next man," he chuckled, dealing with an expert ease that should have alerted her and probably would have if Savannah hadn't convinced herself she was largely unbeatable this evening.

A few moments later Cord turned over his cards with cool expectancy. "Twenty-one," he murmured. "That does indeed leave me the undisputed winner after all, doesn't it? Don't worry, I'll let you nag me over dessert."

"I want another shot at this," Savannah gritted, thoroughly irritated, the reckless feeling growing stronger. She would not let him get away with this. She was bound to win if she tried a couple more times!

"What else have you got to put up for the pot?" he inquired politely, one russet brow lifting.

"I'll . . ." She paused, searching her mind, and then said quickly, "I'll pay for dinner if I lose."

"No good," he said immediately, shaking his head firmly. "That's my privilege."

"I can't think of anything else, dammit! Unless you want to play for real money," she added hopefully.

"Absolutely not. A boss should never gamble for money with his employees. Bad for the image." He waited a moment, watching the shifting expressions on Savannah's frowning features. "You're sure you'll win, given another chance?"

"Of course! I've been winning all evening. This is just a temporary setback!" She had so wanted to flatten him by coming out on top of the silly game. It wasn't fair that the cause of all her romantic troubles was now going to have the satisfaction of beating her at cards! She took another angry sip of wine.

"If you're quite certain of victory," he began smoothly, "I can suggest another bet."

"Yes?" she pressed at once, hope springing up quickly. Savannah leaned forward encouragingly and the light glinted on the gold chain around her neck.

He appeared to be studying the necklace and then he said calmly, "You can wager a kiss."

"A kiss!" she snapped in astonishment.

"Given of your own free will. To be collected by me at a time of my choosing," he explained, eyes full of challenge and mockery.

Savannah took a deep breath, on the verge of telling him to go to hell when a thought struck her. Who said she had to pay off her gambling debts? Furthermore there was a very good chance she wouldn't lose anyway. What did it matter if she wagered something like a kiss? She let the breath escape on a sigh of inner decision. "All right. I agree to the terms of the bet," she stated proudly, her head lifting with instinctive haughtiness.

"You must be feeling lucky, indeed," Cord observed, dealing the cards once more.

"I am," she vowed. And promptly lost. "Are you cheating?" she accused, glaring ferociously. It had all happened so fast! Thank God she had never meant to honor the wager. But still . . .

"Calling a man a cheat at cards used to be grounds for pistols at dawn," he told her, the well-shaped fingers of one hand toying with a queen of hearts. The chill in his voice said more clearly than words that Cordell Harding was not accustomed to being so accused. In spite of herself Savannah lowered her eyes before his and muttered something about not understanding how her luck could have changed so rapidly.

"That's the thing about luck," he advised in that authoritative way he had. "It's highly unpredictable."

Savannah watched mutely for a moment as he neatly stacked the chips and prepared to put the pack of cards back into the cardboard box. She took the last sip of her wine and set the glass down with a ringing clink. It was inconceivable that this man should be the winner tonight. Even if she never intended to honor her bet, she still wanted the satisfaction of winning!

"One more chance, Cord," she pleaded softly, unaware she was using his first name. The tawny eyes gleamed golden and warm across the table at him.

He glanced up from the task of restacking the chips. For a moment he met her eyes without saying anything and then he murmured gently, "I'm thinking it would be wise for me to quit while I'm still ahead," he said coolly, but he ceased stacking the chips.

"I thought you could take a dare," she said tauntingly, leaning forward once again, resting both elbows on the table, and cradling her chin on her folded hands. "Besides," she argued, "the whole point of this was for me to win, remember?" She waited, feeling a curious tension mount between them as Cord considered the situation. She gave him a tiny half-smile of anticipation.

"What can you offer me?" he whispered in a deeply male way. A way that clearly said he wasn't interested in playing for matchsticks. The gray-green eyes pinned her, and for a fleeting moment Savannah was put forcibly to mind of a large cat stalking its prey. The sensation sent a small shiver down her backbone, but she refused to pay it any heed. It no longer mattered what she wagered, she thought grimly. She had no intention of settling the debt. Winning was the only thing in her mind at the moment. Winning so big that Cord Harding would acknowledge himself a complete loser. All the anger and frustration she had experienced from the loss of Jeff was boiling to a climax inside and she badly wanted someone to pay. There was no way to punish Jeff, but Cord . . .

"You set the terms of the bet," she suggested, her words barely audible.

"All or nothing again?"

"Yes," she agreed, the tip of her tongue touching the corner of her mouth in a tiny betrayal of her inner tension and nervousness. It was the only sign.

He waited a couple of heartbeats and then rasped, "If I'm to set the terms, there's no reason I shouldn't have you bet something I very badly wish to win."

Savannah's sleek head tilted slightly and she waited, not disagreeing.

"Would you pay off, I wonder?" he said half to himself. It was the first time he had implied he had some doubts on that matter.

"As you told me a few minutes ago, that sort of accusation would have been cause for a duel not so long ago," she responded with a touch of formality to hide her start of surprise.

"I apologize," he said, equally formally, inclining his head politely.

"The terms of the wager?" she prompted, trying to conceal her eagerness.

"This is Friday night," he noted irrelevantly as far as Savannah was concerned.

She simply nodded her head, waiting.

"If I win," he said, making each word count heavily, watching her face to see the effect, "you will spend the weekend with me. Beginning with dinner tonight."

In the incredulous silence that followed, Savannah felt the blood drain from her face in shock. She couldn't believe she had heard correctly! Another kiss, a date, something along those lines she had been prepared for. She could hardly comprehend the audacity of the man! Who the hell did he think he was? It took every ounce of will she possessed to stifle her inner rage as she sat back in her chair and stared at Cord with a measure of fascination.

"You're joking," she finally bit out hoarsely.

"No."

"You expect me to accept a bet like that?" she breathed, eyes full of golden fire.

"It depends on how badly you wish to play another round of cards, I suppose," he said casually. "You surely can't expect me to jeopardize my winnings for something trivial. The stake must be something I want."

"And you think a weekend with me is something you want?" she asked unbelievingly.

"I think it would be time well spent," he confirmed, the ghost of a smile touching his mouth. His right hand ruffled the deck of cards enticingly and Savannah's gaze was drawn to the unimportant action. "Of course, we can always end the game here and now. . . ."

"With you the undisputed winner?" Savannah lifted her chin regally.

"I'm capable of being a gracious victor and don't forget you're going to get a free meal out of this." The curve of his mouth widened. "You'll find that losing to me isn't such a terrible experience," he drawled.

Nothing could have managed to grate on her nerves at that moment as thoroughly as Cord's masculine amusement. Quite suddenly it came to Savannah that if she did, indeed, play for such high stakes Cord Harding would be punished regardless of whether she won or lost. If she won, she could get up and walk away from the table with the pleasure of seeing him soundly defeated. If she lost—heaven forbid!—she would still have the pleasure of welshing on her bet. It might be nearly as satisfying to lead him into thinking she was going to spend an entire weekend with him and then staging a neat disappearance!

Taking a firm grip on her courage and prodding herself with a great deal of emotion-induced rationalization, Savannah swallowed and then, very bravely, nodded her head in a short, brief acceptance of the terms of the wager.

"You agree to the bet?" he asked, as if making completely certain.

"I agree," she stated coldly, trying to sound utterly and sophisticatedly casual about the whole thing.

"You'll forgive me if I fail to do the sporting thing and wish you good luck?" he said gently, picking up the cards and beginning to shuffle. His eyes never left hers.

Savannah didn't say a word, but she lowered her own eyes as soon as the cards had been dealt. She wanted so badly to win this game! The concentration she was exerting furrowed her forehead, drawing the lines of her eyebrows together over the straight nose as she carefully examined her hand. The numbers were too low. She would have to try one more card and hope not to exceed the magic figure of twenty-one.

Cord was equally silent, assessing his own hand and responding to her call for another card without saying a word.

Eighteen. She would have to stand pat and pray Cord would draw too high. . . . Savannah glanced up anxiously as he drew a card. She saw the flicker of satisfaction in his eyes a second before he turned over his cards and she knew she had lost.

"Twenty-one," he submitted in an almost gentle way, watching her expression as he displayed his hand. His own face gave no indication of his emotions other than the hint of contentment she saw in his eyes before a shuttered look took its place.

Savannah turned over her own cards without a word and quickly thrust her fingers down into her lap and out of sight. She didn't want Cord to see how they were shaking. *Relax,* she told herself furiously. *Nothing all that dreadful has happened. You'll*

28

still have the pleasure of denying the victor his winnings. . . .

"I would like to leave now," Cord said abruptly, getting to his feet without bothering to restack the cards.

Savannah's eyes flew to his as he came around to her side of the table and took hold of her arm in an outward show of gentlemanly behavior. But there was steel beneath the velvet touch, and Savannah knew at once it would be useless to protest.

And if the truth were known, she acknowledged ruefully as he guided her easily through the cheerful, curious crowd, right now she needed the physical support. She wasn't at all certain she could have walked that gauntlet of interested eyes on her own.

CHAPTER TWO

"You did that very well," Cord approved as they emerged from Mel's home into the balmy Southern California evening. "Like a queen." He slanted an emerald glance down at her, but Savannah kept her own gaze proudly ahead. Under the influence of fresh air and the warmth of a setting summer sun, reason was beginning to return to her. What the devil had gotten into her to make her play such a silly game!

"What are you talking about?" she snapped resentfully, her mind beginning to churn. He was leading her toward a subtly toned Mercedes parked on the street. A new one.

"The rather magnificent way you just left that party," he grinned suddenly. "If it gives you any satisfaction, Jeff Painter was staring quite openly in astonishment."

"Along with everyone else, I imagine! Not exactly the most dignified exit I've ever made."

"But undoubtedly one of the more memorable. Where did you park your car?"

"I came with Maria, the other woman in the personnel department," Savannah admitted, badly wishing she'd brought her own car. It would have been an excellent excuse for separating from him long enough to drive off into the sunset. Well, she would just have to think of a more clever way to escape him before the evening was over. Tomorrow she would be leaving for her vacation, something Cord Harding would have no way of knowing since he didn't choose to involve himself in such petty details as the timing of employee vacations. The loss this evening at cards was humiliating but it would be vastly pleasant to walk out on Cord after leading him to think she intended to spend an entire weekend with him! My God! What an opinion he must have had of her!

"That makes it easy then, doesn't it?" he smiled, opening the door of the Mercedes and giving her a gentle push when she didn't automatically slide onto the leather seat. "We'll just take my car." He slammed the door with an air of finality.

Her fingers were still shaking, Savannah noted almost dispassionately, glancing down at her folded hands in her lap. She wondered if Cord had noticed. She must *think!*

"I know a nice little place where the abalone is guaranteed fresh," Cord said, glancing into his side

32

mirror before pulling away from the curb. "And the wine cellar is excellent. Sound good?"

"Not particularly," she answered truthfully, wondering if he would give up on making her enjoy the evening if she proved obstinate enough.

"Feeling bitter?" he asked. "You'll be much more cheerful after a good meal of abalone and that nice, crisp white wine Antonio just got in. . . ."

"You do this sort of thing regularly?" she demanded disbelievingly, wondering how he could seem so casual about the whole thing.

"Gamble with a woman for stakes like this? Nope. This is a first for me," he chuckled, shifting gears with expertise. "What about you? Are you normally this reckless or only when you're mad at the world?"

"Don't be ridiculous," she hissed, refusing to look at him. Perhaps the easiest thing to do would be to wait until dinner was over and then excuse herself to go to the ladies' room. She could walk out of the restaurant and find a phone. . . .

"But you are angry tonight, aren't you, Savannah?" he asked delicately. "You're not in tears over Jeff Painter, you're just madder than hell. Doesn't that tell you anything?"

"Would you rather I cry?" she demanded tightly. "The only thing I could shed tears over is the way you won at cards tonight!"

"Perhaps that means your luck has changed. If you're now unlucky in cards, you'll be lucky in love. Isn't that how it goes?" he asked with the dismaying air of someone determined to make another see the bright side of life.

"Then the opposite must be true for you," she pointed out sweetly. "You're due for a turn of bad luck in love now, aren't you?" *And you'll get it tonight,* she thought determinedly, *when I walk out on you!*

"Ah, but you see, I don't believe in luck, except insofar as a man makes his own. But something tells me we'll make a very fortunate pair. . . ."

"For a weekend?" He certainly wasn't making any attempt to imply that he intended a long-term relationship, Savannah thought furiously. Talk about adding insult to injury!

"For a weekend," he agreed. "On Sunday night we'll discuss the future."

"You're very callous about the whole thing," she noted aloofly, wanting to reach out and wrap her fingers around his throat for thinking of her in such casual terms. Of course there was always the fact that she had agreed to the horrid bet. Perhaps he couldn't be blamed completely for his actions. He was, after all, merely a typical male, willing to take advantage of a situation. Perhaps the touch of novelty in this particular circumstance attracted him too.

"I'm trying to be as cool as yourself," he smiled wryly.

Savannah ignored that and every other attempt Cord made at conversation until he had located the restaurant, they were seated in an intimate booth, and the menus had been distributed.

"Am I going to get the silent treatment all weekend?" he inquired at one point after Savannah had opened her mouth only to give her order to the wait-

34

er. He studied her tense expression, and the gray-green gaze flickered with a combination of amusement and male anticipation.

"There was nothing in the terms of the bet that said I have to be chatty," she said distantly, staring at the wine in her glass and telling herself she wasn't going to have another drop that evening.

"True, but I somehow thought you'd be a more gracious loser."

"Why?" she asked, frowning ferociously at him.

"I don't know." He mused slowly. "I suppose because you're always so quick to smile at people and talk to them."

"It's part of my job." She shrugged.

"As is lecturing the boss on proper management techniques?" He chuckled warmly.

"I've never lectured you . . ." she began defensively, only to have him use a fork to wave her to silence.

"Yes, you have," he declared stoutly. "There's your running battle with me over the concerns of the employees' club, the skirmish you waged to get the company to pay employee tuition fees for classes that could barely be said to be job-related, the argument you made to persuade me to let all female employees miss an hour and a half of work two weeks ago to attend a rape prevention seminar . . ."

"A very *useful* class, incidentally," she stated meaningfully.

"Don't you dare threaten me, Savannah Emery," Cord warned, equally meaningfully. "I won this weekend fair and square and you have no right at all to cry rape. Especially when you know damn good and well I'd never resort to that kind of brutality."

"How do I know that?" she shot back, goaded.

"You'd never have gone so far as to play cards with a man you distrusted that thoroughly," he announced, as if stating the obvious.

She blinked at him resentfully.

"You look like an irritated little cat when you do that." He suddenly grinned.

"What?" she grumbled.

"Blink those big gold eyes at me like that. Oh, good, here comes the abalone," he added cheerfully, spotting the waiter bearing down on them with a loaded tray. "You'll feel better when you've had a good meal. Afterward we'll get in a little dancing in the lounge—"

"And then what?" she asked daringly, trying to decide when it would be best to make her break.

"Why, then I'll take you home, of course," he returned blandly. "Home to my place, that is, where I'll find out what it takes to make a little cat like you purr." He smiled at her with such outrageous intent that Savannah seriously considered using her table knife on him. Then it struck her that he had used the adjective *little*. To describe her! Some traitorous part of her mind began to forget about Jeff and wonder what it would be like to dance with a man who was large enough to make her feel tiny and fragile like—like that Alison person over whom Jeff had gone crazy.

"You seem very sure now that I'll pay my gambling debts," she murmured, thinking that ever since

36

they had left the party Cord had appeared more relaxed. And that, she decided intuitively, was probably the best frame of mind in which to keep him. She didn't want any hitches when she finally decided to end the evening.

"I think," he retorted in a deep, intimate voice, "that now that I've got you in reach, I can make you *want* to pay your debts!"

With sudden decision Savannah decided to play the evening for all it was worth. If Cord Harding was egotistical enough to think he could make her relish the paying of this particular debt, he deserved everything he was going to get. Even if she weren't doing this for revenge, she would still go through with her plans, she told herself stoutly. She owed it to the next female in his life.

"Have you given much thought to the practicalities of the situation?" she ventured dryly. "There's the little matter of my clothes . . ."

"We can stop by your place on the way to the beach tomorrow," he told her cheerily, cutting a bite of abalone with obvious pleasure. "You won't need anything else tonight."

Savannah bit her lip in an effort not to yell at him that he had no right to treat her so cavalierly. She no longer knew whether the pink in her cheeks was caused by anger or embarrassment. Did he really think she would let two men treat her so shabbily in the course of one evening? The fact that she might have aided and abetted the situation by allowing herself to be drawn into such a dangerous pastime as gambling with a man like this no longer mattered. Cord Harding was going to learn a lesson tonight.

"You seem to have the whole weekend planned already," she forced herself to say with a touch of admiration. "The beach tomorrow, you said?" She dug into her baked potato as if mining it for some precious metal. The activity gave her something else to do with her hands besides throwing things across the table. It also meant she didn't have to meet that fascinating, incredibly insistent gaze.

"Would you like that? I know a private little cove down the coast a ways where we could swim and picnic and"—he paused significantly before adding carefully—"amuse ourselves. Then I thought we would spend the next night somewhere along the coast. One of the small towns between here and San Diego. On Sunday afternoon we'll drive leisurely back, and Sunday evening we'll have our little talk about the future," he concluded in the competent way he would rough out the agenda of a business meeting.

"Tell me," she asked after a moment's consideration, "when, exactly, did you determine this schedule?" She glanced up and found him watching her intently.

"If I told you, you'd probably be furious," he admitted ruefully, the amusement plain in his expression.

"You think I'm not already thoroughly incensed over the entire matter?" she asked sweetly.

He laughed at that, a rich, pleasant rumble that began somewhere in the expanse of his chest. "Good

38

point. Okay, I'll tell you the truth. I planned the weekend or something close to it the moment you accepted my invitation to gamble this evening!"

Savannah stared at him. "So you did cheat!" she exclaimed, throwing down her napkin and starting to rise to her feet. She needed no other excuse now.

He met her glaring, flaming eyes, and the laughter died in his own. "Sit down," he said very softly in a voice she had heard him use rarely and only in highly unpleasant situations. She sat, surprised at her own behavior. It must have had something to do with the psychological fact that her mind still thought of him as the boss, she decided unhappily.

"That's the second time this evening you've accused me of cheating," he stated coldly. "I think you owe me an apology. Just as I apologized to you for implying you might not honor your gambling debts."

"I'm not in the mood to apologize," she hissed, aware of the impact of his displeasure. "I've had what has amounted to the worst evening of my entire life and I'm not going to say I'm sorry for any impolite remarks that may slip out from time to time."

He folded his arms on the table in front of his plate, the crisp whiteness of his long-sleeved shirt gleaming brighter than the linen on the table. "I'm to be prepared for such remarks all weekend?"

"You surely didn't expect me to be generous in defeat, did you?"

"Not, perhaps, at the beginning of the evening, but by tomorrow morning, yes. I think you will be in a much better temper then." He smiled with cool promise, his eyes softening once more. "I'll let your insult pass for the moment. You can apologize later. Finish your meal and we'll adjourn to the lounge."

"Yes, Mr. Harding," she retorted in a saucy imitation of the way she would have agreed to his demands at the office.

"That's right." He nodded approvingly. "Keep reminding yourself that I'm the one in charge and we won't have any serious difficulties."

Savannah let one loftily raised eyebrow convey her reaction to his outrageous remark before picking up her fork and attacking the remains of her abalone.

It wasn't until they had left the table and Cord had procured a small place in the lounge that Savannah decided to put step one of her hastily concocted plan into action.

"Would you excuse me a moment?" she said politely, in the manner women have always used to announce they are going to the ladies' room.

Cord slanted a glance up at her as she got to her feet and then nodded his head briefly. What else could a man do in such circumstances? Savannah thought, pleased with the simple ruse. But an uncomfortable feeling between her shoulders as she walked sedately across the darkened lounge told her he was watching. Fortunately she wouldn't have to take the risk of walking toward the lobby of the restaurant. The telephone was in an area adjacent to the restrooms, and all Cord could see from his vantage point was that she had gone in the proper direction to find the facilities.

Once around the corner and out of sight, Savannah picked up her skirts and flew toward the pay

40

phone on the wall. Yanking open the yellow pages of the phone book, she madly scrambled for the taxi listings, found one, and dialed with fingers that trembled ever so slightly.

"I can have a cab there in about fifteen minutes," a bored dispatcher informed her after she'd given her location.

"That will be fine," she breathed thankfully. Fifteen minutes from now she would have to find another excuse to leave Cord, but something useful would come to mind, she was certain. She hung up the phone and, lifting her chin determinedly, walked back toward the lounge.

A band had begun to play and Cord rose politely to his feet as she approached. "Just in time for the first dance," he said, reaching for her elbow. "Here, you can leave your purse on the table. I'm sure it will be safe."

Without a word Savannah followed him acquiescently onto the floor, finding that when he took her into his arms she was in an ideal position to glance at the digital watch on her wrist from time to time without being obvious about it. Fifteen minutes . . .

She was right about one thing, she decided almost instantly. It was very pleasant dancing with a full-sized man! Not that Jeff Painter was scrawny by any means, she tacked on mentally, feeling guilty. But he didn't have the height and breadth of shoulder with which Cord Harding had been blessed. Almost unconsciously Savannah began to relax. She loved

41

dancing and with her innate grace it came easily to her.

"You dance exactly as I imagined you would," Cord whispered huskily into her ear as he led her slowly around the floor. "All soft and flowing in my arms. Such a charming combination of female characteristics in you, my little queen," he went on caressingly, using his hand to push her head carefully down on his shoulder. Savannah realized suddenly that the evening's calculated seduction had begun, and she felt a curious tension quicken within herself. The new, instinctive alertness didn't affect her dancing but it made her uncomfortably aware of every aspect of Cord Harding. The same awareness the hunted had of the hunter.

"I knew Painter was the wrong man for you the moment I saw the pair of you together," Cord went on, clearly satisfied as to the correctness of his analysis. Savannah felt his fingers probing the sensitive line of her spine where it curved at the small of her back. She shifted her position ever so slightly in an effort to escape the intimate touch and found herself closer than ever against his lean, hard length. She also sensed his satisfaction in having her close the distance between them and could have kicked herself.

"You can't know anything about the situation between myself and Jeff," she protested icily, lifting her head from his shoulder and sneaking a glance at the face of her watch.

"I've had to learn a lot about people in the course of my life." He smiled in polite disagreement. "And you, with your excellent record in personnel work, should have had the sense to see what I saw."

"And what great revelation were you privileged to see that I missed?" she taunted, not quite meeting his eyes. She wished he wouldn't hold her so close. The absolutely false impressions of safety and security and tightly leashed passion her body was picking up from his were dangerous in the extreme.

"That you're much too strong for him. He needs someone like that sweet little Alison What's-her-name. You would have overwhelmed him, Savannah. Can't you see that? Just as I'd guess you've probably managed to overwhelm most of the men in your life. . . ."

"I trust you won't make the mistake of thinking I'm going to take that remark as flattering!"

His predatory smile widened. "But I meant it as a compliment, Savannah. I hate insipid people whose emotions are lukewarm at best. Men admire you, that's plain to see, because they're attracted to the warmth in your smile and the promise of adventure in those strange eyes of yours. But when they get close, most of them are going to decide it's safer to keep you as a friend rather than as a lover. Jeff would have come to the same conclusion eventually, even if he hadn't got himself shipped off to San Diego."

"He was falling in love with me!" she argued in a stiff little voice.

"He was attracted to you," Cord corrected flatly. "And I'll admit you had him going there for a while. If nothing had interfered, you might have convinced him to become engaged, but sooner or later you

43

would have ruined things by losing your temper or demanding too much of him. If you hadn't been so set on pursuing your goal of making him fall in love with you, I'm sure your normal common sense would have told you he was ultimately going to be much too weak and uninteresting for you."

"And you think I'm going to see the light this weekend and realize I need someone more like you?" she rasped, infuriated at the depths of his male conceit.

"We're two of a kind, Savannah," he murmured placatingly, the strong fingers moving tantalizingly on her back.

"I'm supposed to be tempted into a weekend affair by that kind of statement?"

"It needn't end this weekend," he drawled deliberately, his grip tightening.

"But it will," she challenged. "You're not fooling me, Cord. I've seen the look in your eyes tonight in the eyes of other men in the past. A woman doesn't reach my age without having learned something about the opposite sex, unless she's very stupid. You've found yourself in the novel position of having won a woman for a weekend and you're thinking it would be pleasant to get what you can while you can."

"Is there anything wrong with old-fashioned male need and desire?" he grated in a slightly thickened voice. "I'm only a man, Savannah, and I'm subject to the same drives as other men. The main difference with me is that I recognize the fact it takes a woman like you to satisfy me."

44

Savannah had to admire his approach. It certainly was different from that of her usual dates and equally different from Jeff Painter's mild pursuit. She imagined Cord had a great deal of success with his particular line. What woman wouldn't respond to the notion that she was somehow unique? Too bad he had to go and spoil things by admitting that what he felt was simply masculine desire. He should have added a bit of polish to the approach when he used it on women like her.

"Would you like a piece of advice?" she inquired politely.

"What's that?" he demanded warily.

"The next time you're trying to seduce a woman by telling her how much you lust after her, try softening the edges of your line a little. You know, imply that your heart is just the tiniest bit involved, not just your male instincts!"

"But then she'd think I was lying through my teeth, wouldn't she?" he retorted, the gray-green eyes full of mockery and something else. Something primitive, which made Savannah deeply glad she had a cab arriving in just a few minutes.

"Perhaps," she agreed with a small gurgle of laughter. There was a definite sense of intoxication to be derived from the experience of bantering with a man like Cord. Especially when one knew escape was close at hand.

"I'd rather the situation between us be an honest one," he asked, his eyes narrowing at the sound of her laughter. "I'd prefer you not to think I'm lying. . . ."

45

She lifted one shoulder in a graphic attempt to let him know it didn't matter to her whether or not he was lying, and before he could respond, the music came to an end. None too soon, either, Savannah realized, risking another quick glance at her watch. She really should be on her way.

Her nerves keying to a new pitch of tension, Savannah slipped into the chair Cord held for her and reached automatically to pick up her purse. He was lowering himself into the seat opposite when she opened the small catch and pretended to fish around inside.

"Uh-oh," she murmured mildly, trying not to overdo it. She let a hint of a frown touch her forehead as she bent industriously over the purse's contents.

"What's wrong?" he asked.

"Nothing serious. I left my lipstick in the ladies' room. I'd better run and get it before someone picks it up or throws it in the trash. I'll just be a moment. . . ." Without waiting for a response, she rose quickly and smiled at him inquiringly, as if seeking his permission to leave. He nodded politely and she was off, hurrying in the direction she had gone before. It would be safer to use that back service entrance she had spotted earlier, she had decided during the course of the dance. She didn't want to rouse Cord's suspicions by heading for the lobby area.

A busboy and a waitress, obviously enjoying a little dalliance in a dark corner during a break, glanced up curiously as Savannah slipped past them, but neither said anything as she opened the back door and stepped out into the rear parking lot. Clos-

46

ing the door behind her, she hastened around to the front of the large building and there, right on time, stood a waiting cab.

What stopped her from dashing forward at once wasn't the sight of the taxi. It was the sight of the tall, red-haired man bending down to stuff some cash through the driver's open window. Cord! But that was impossible! She had just left him seated in the lounge. He would have had to walk straight out the front door the moment she headed toward the rest-room area!

At that moment he turned and saw her standing in the glare of the parking-lot floodlights, her skirts held in one hand and an expression of frustrated astonishment on her face. He smiled. Never had the impression of a large, dangerous predator been so clear.

Savannah felt a cold fury sweep through her as Cord paced deliberately forward, the driver of the taxi behind him pulling out of the lot without a backward glance.

"There you are, my dear," Cord said in a satiny voice that flicked along her nerves as no tone of outright anger could have succeeded in doing. "Ready to leave, I see. I'm pleased you're as anxious to pursue the rest of the evening's entertainment as I am." He was angry but not infuriated, Savannah could tell. Not like she was.

She remembered to close her open mouth with a small snap of frustration and lifted her head haughtily as he approached to take her arm in a grip of iron.

"A nice try, Savannah," he assured her evenly as he guided her toward the Mercedes. "But I really couldn't let you get away with it. Debts of honor must be paid, you see."

"What makes you think that taxi was waiting for me?" she shot back savagely. Damn him! She would defeat him at his own game, she swore silently. Instead of digging in her heels right here in the parking lot, she would find a way to escape tonight that was as thoroughly humiliating as she could manage! She would pay him back for his presumption if it was the last thing she did!

"I beg your pardon," he said at once. "I'm afraid I assumed . . ." He let the sentence trail off on a mocking note.

"You assumed incorrectly, then," she retorted acidly. "Why would I want to run away from the opportunity of being seduced by the president of the firm? Especially when he's gone to such lengths to assure me his intentions are dishonorable. Of course it means I shall have to start looking for work on Monday, but—"

"What makes you say that?" he interrupted, startled, as he opened the car door and settled her firmly inside.

"Office affairs are always so embarrassing when they end," she explained kindly as he followed her down onto the seat, crowding her into the corner. "And in the case of one between a female employee and the head of the company, others always feel so sorry for the woman that humiliation finally forces her to quit. Assuming she has some pride, that is."

He hesitated before replying, starting the engine with a vicious gesture and throwing the expensive vehicle into reverse. "That excuse won't be any more effective than the taxi-escape plan was," he informed her eventually as he pulled out onto the street. But he wasn't looking at her, and Savannah was left with the impression she had surprised him.

"No, I imagine not," she agreed on a sigh. "I expect it's a simple matter to hire equally qualified people to take my position. After all, there must be zillions of unemployed personnel types out there looking for work." She waved a hand at the neon-lit cityscape around them.

"We'll discuss the matter Sunday night," he retorted distantly, concentrating on his driving.

And in that moment it came to Savannah that she really was going to have to quit. Not Monday, naturally. Monday she would be on vacation. But as soon as she returned in two weeks she would hand in her notice. What else could she do after this evening's fiasco? Even though she intended to escape relatively unscathed, she would never be able to face working with this man again! She had never before managed to embroil herself in such a ridiculous situation as this and she told herself to take a lesson from it. Wine and cards and emotions didn't go well together!

Cord's home proved to be an attractive condominium in a quiet neighborhood of tastefully designed homes. The style was California modern, which meant a lot of glass and angles and just a hint of the Spanish touch. But the overall effect would have been pleasing to Savannah if she hadn't been so thoroughly immersed in her own thoughts. The Mercedes was to be left ungaraged, she noted as Cord parked the car and walked around to open the door for her. Now she must pay attention to what he did with the keys. . . .

Without a word she allowed herself to be led up the brick walk, where Cord used the same ring of keys on which the Mercedes key resided to open the door. As he indicated she should precede him into the wide, tiled hall, the ring of keys was inserted carelessly into the drawer of a small wooden stand nearby. She was surprised by his lack of caution and feeling quite jubilant over it when she turned to find him watching her with such uncompromising desire that she automatically took a step backward.

She realized what was happening and for the first time a tingle of genuine fear found its way into the mainstream of her emotions, taking its place alongside the anger and determination to escape. Cord wasn't thinking about hiding his keys because he only had one thing on his mind at the moment. And Cord Harding could be extraordinarily single-minded at times.

"I think," he stated as if coming to a momentous decision, "that I will collect my payments from you in the order in which I won them. I've had dinner with you and now I want the kiss you wagered." There was an emerald fire flaring in the depths of his eyes, a fire that threatened to leap fully into life and consume both of them. Savannah felt the palms of her hands grow moist as the tension in the room seemed to feed on itself, making her feel incredibly and uncustomarily weak.

"Cord, no, I . . ." she began instinctively holding up a hand in a futile attempt to ward him off. She frowned severely at him.

"Come now, little queen," he coaxed gently, closing the distance between them with sure, intent steps. "The first payment wasn't so bad, was it? You ate every scrap of food," he reminded her, and she wanted to laugh hysterically at the irrelevance of the remark. "All I'm asking at the moment is the kiss you owe me. After that I'll make us some coffee and we can talk for a time. I won't rush you, I swear. . . ." He broke off encouragingly and Savannah was shocked to find herself responding to the reassurance in his voice. Coffee, she thought desperately, when he went to make coffee she would have a chance at the keys. That meant giving him his kiss, putting him off guard.

The fingers of her outstretched hand closed into a small fist and Savannah lowered it to her side. "You can have your kiss," she offered icily, as if granting him a great favor. She stood her ground as he reached out to take hold of her by the shoulders.

"Thank you," he murmured politely. "I was going to take it regardless of your feelings on the subject."

Savannah had an instant, dizzying impression of having got much too close to the source of the emerald fire in his eyes, and then his mouth was on hers in a hungry, exploring, exultant kiss that took away her breath with the force of its demand.

Never had she experienced a kiss like this! It was

an amazingly accurate reflection of the man himself. Large, powerful, dominant. With the ruthless curiosity of an invader in a strange land, Cord searched the territory of her mouth, demolishing resistance where he found it and widening the scope of his authority until she found herself trying to stop him from the final invasion by clamping her teeth tightly together.

"I want a proper kiss," he grated warningly, his mouth hovering momentarily above hers as he used his thumb to probe the corner of her lips until he had forced them apart. When he took them again he pressed his nail very carefully into the vulnerable flesh and Savannah jumped, startled.

"Ouch!" she got out in a faint protest, and then he was inside, consolidating his victory and tasting the warm sweetness that he'd won.

CHAPTER THREE

Instinct prompted Savannah's reaction to Cord's overwhelming assault, a very feminine instinct that cautioned that she couldn't hope to fight him. He was so much stronger than she and his strength was augmented by the force of a masculine will that Savannah realized would only be intensified by resistance. And besides, she rationalized as she deliberately let herself relax in his arms, didn't she want to put him off guard? Make him so certain of her compliance that he would unthinkingly provide the break she needed to escape?

"Savannah, my sweet Savannah," Cord breathed on a sigh of sheer male pleasure as he felt her soften within the confines of his hold. "I've waited so long to kiss you, touch you. . . ." He freed her lips to investigate the sensitive area behind her ear, nuzzling the line of her throat while his hands slid to the curve of her hips and he pulled her tightly against him.

"But, Cord!" she gasped, chillingly aware of the rising need in him. "We—we hardly know each other. How can you say you've wanted me for longer than an—an evening?" Her hands, which had gone initially to his shoulders in a futile try at holding him away from her, moved over the whiteness of his expensive shirt, the tips of her fingers unconsciously kneading the smoothly muscled skin underneath. It would be amusing to let him think he was sweeping her off her feet with the force of his passion, Savannah told herself, sensing his response to her touch.

"An evening, a few days, weeks—what does it matter?" He pressed against the warmth of her shoulder as he used one hand to pull aside the soft cowl neckline of her dress. A tremor went through him as he caressed her, and she wondered at the strangeness of a man's desire. "When a man suddenly realizes he wants a woman very badly, time isn't important. I swear that before this night is over you'll want me as much as I want you, little queen. By tomorrow morning you won't even be able to remember what that fool Painter looks like!"

"You're so sure of yourself," she cried on a small sob of frustration and—heaven help her!—desire. She must control herself and the situation. Everything depended on that now. "Do you always get what you want, Cord Harding?" She closed her eyes, resting her head against the strong shoulder, and tried desperately to think. It was clear to her now that she had somehow become a challenge to him.

For some reason Cord Harding had decided to amuse himself with her, prove how easy it was to make a woman forget another man. Damn him!

"If I want it badly enough," he told her unhesitatingly, the certainty in his words a weapon itself. How did a woman combat that kind of arrogance? "And I do want you, Savannah Emery. I could hardly believe it tonight when you let your anger and desire for revenge push you into that last bet," he exulted, his pleasure in her stupidity very plain. "Such a foolish little cat, so sure you would come out ahead! Thank God it was me you were playing with and not some idiot who wouldn't have had the sense to know what he'd won."

The hand he had used to push aside her dress dropped caressingly down the length of her side, the fingers sliding possessively over the shape of her breast. He groaned, a husky sound of male desire, and Savannah was horrified to discover the extent of her own reaction. A part of her was stirring, responding to Cord's implicit demands, and when his hand halted just under the weight of her breast, it was she who trembled.

"You won't be sorry, sweetheart," he murmured, shifting his stance in a way that finally alerted Savannah's rapidly deteriorating common sense. If she was ever going to act, it had better be right now!

"Cord, please!" she whispered, trying frantically to infuse her soft plea with a sense of genuine appeal. Intuition guided her and she knew she had nothing better to depend upon at that moment. "You promised we . . . could talk." She gazed up at him with

55

the wide, soft eyes of a woman who is in danger of becoming overwhelmed with the passion of the moment. The only thing that disturbed Savannah was that it wasn't all an act. It was more than a little frightening to discover one's vulnerability in a man's arms. Jeff's kisses had never affected her in quite this way, and it was infuriating to have a man like Cord demonstrate so graphically that there were new horizons to be discovered in the field of love.

"You said you wouldn't rush me," she went on persuasively, feeling him hesitate. The breathlessness of her voice appalled her. Never had she known herself to sound so weak and helpless. That knowledge, more than anything else, gave her the strength to stand firm. She was not a silly female to be swept off her feet by the forceful, undisguised desire of a man! She was capable of controlling her own emotions.

"We can talk later, my sweet Savannah," he promised, his lips trailing a line of fiery little kisses back to her mouth. "Later, after you know just how much I want you and mean to have you. . . ."

"Please," she begged, sensing his determination. "I need some time, Cord. This is all happening so fast. I won't fight you," she added, lying gently as she lowered her eyes in feminine submission. "But you did say you wouldn't rush me." She tried a tiny bit of force, pushing carefully against his shoulders, trying to put some distance between herself and the rock-hard body against which she was being held. She almost felt him making a decision and held her breath, wondering what the outcome would be.

Then, to her vast relief, he allowed her to step away from him, although he didn't free her.

"You're begging me to give you time and I want to plead with you to let me rush you," he said with a crooked little smile. She sensed his deliberate effort to bring his passion under control.

"You promised," she reminded him yet again on a slim thread of sound, her tawny eyes fixed appealingly on his face.

"Do you always hold a man to his promises?" he asked whimsically, tracing the line of her cheek with one rough finger.

She nodded, afraid to say anything.

"Then I haven't much choice, have I?" he decided ruefully. "Just remember," he cautioned gently, "that turnabout is fair play. I shall hold you to your word too."

Savannah ignored the spark of unease that moved deep in her mind and summoned a shaky smile. "You—you included a cup of coffee in the deal, as I recall. . . ."

"You're determined to make me stick by the letter of the contract, aren't you?" He grinned wryly. "Why is that, I wonder? Are you nervous, my reckless lady gambler?"

"A little," she admitted readily, her eyes focusing on the second button of his shirt. She didn't mind him knowing. In addition to being nothing less than the truth, there was a chance he would take things slowly if he thought she was uncertain.

"There's no need," he purred, a dragon's purr that ruffled the edges of her awareness all the way to the

tips of her fingers. Savannah was beginning to realize there was more than one kind of danger involved here, but a tinge of the same daring mood that had led her into the crazy wager still seemed to be at work. *Tomorrow morning,* she thought obliquely, *I'm going to wonder what got into me tonight.*
. . ..

"Regardless of whatever impression you may have received this evening," she told Cord, "I don't make a habit of playing for the kind of stakes we played for tonight. Everything happened so quickly that I'm—"

"Still not sure how you come to find yourself in my arms?" he concluded, tugging her closer again and bending to drop a warm, tantalizing kiss on her slightly parted lips. Savannah, expecting another full-scale attack, was thrown off balance by the gentleness in this caress. She stared up at him as he raised his head again, and the gray-green eyes smiled back at her with that waiting look she had seen in them earlier.

"You're here," he went on beguilingly, "because I want you here and because I think you want to be here. Don't you, Savannah? Why not tell me the truth, my sweet? You would never have risked that last bet tonight if you hadn't wanted to risk losing to me. Your pride would never have allowed you to simply tell me you wanted to go home with me. But in a game of chance you could throw your fate to the winds."

Savannah heard the complete male satisfaction in his words and it restored whatever faltering determination she was experiencing. This man was going to get a lesson tonight. It was merely a matter of time, she swore silently while turning a deliberately feminine smile up at him.

"Perhaps I took the chance because I never expected you to insist on payment," she suggested a little dryly, twisting out of his grasp with a graceful turn.

"You know me better than that," he chuckled softly. "Two months of having worked for me must have taught you I always follow through on a deal. Why don't you relax and admit the truth to both of us?" There was a gentle persuasion about him that tugged at her, even though Savannah's mind was firmly decided.

She walked away from him, toward the living room, absorbing the rich, warm Spanish decor with its heavy leather furniture, beamed ceilings, and stone fireplace. "You have a lovely home," she remarked, glancing back at him over her shoulder while she paused to examine a woven wall hanging.

"Thank you, but you're not going to sidetrack me," he said easily, following behind her. She could feel his eyes on her body and had to stifle a shiver. It was a heady game, this business of playing with Cord Harding. A game unlike any other she had ever tried. Her relationships with men tended to be of a much different nature, and never in a million years would she have classified herself as a tease. But tonight she felt quite daring, high on a recklessness that she already knew she would regret tomorrow. There was something about this man that was bringing out a side of her nature she had never known existed.

"I wasn't trying to deflect the question," she assured him. "But you're asking a lot by insisting that I admit to an overpowering desire. Leave me some pride, Cord," she begged.

"It will be my pleasure to make you forget your foolish pride before this weekend is over," he vowed, stepping close. "By Sunday night we will be able to be honest with each other."

"You're so sure of yourself," she breathed, torn by rueful admiration for his persistence and a fierce desire to take him down a peg.

"You'll know what I'm talking about soon enough. You're already beginning to understand, aren't you, sweet Savannah?" He touched her neatly coiled hair and she had the impression he would like to have taken it down and run his fingers through it. "I felt it in your kiss a moment ago. I was fairly certain of it at the restaurant when you didn't yell for the taxi to wait. You were relieved, weren't you, when I realized you were plotting and moved to take care of matters. Don't worry, I know you had to make some attempt to run. Your pride probably demanded it. And perhaps you were beginning to be somewhat scared of what you'd done. The wine and your anger at Jeff Painter were both wearing off . . ."

To be replaced by an anger at you that hasn't begun to thin, Savannah finished mentally. "You seem to know me very well," she whispered, lowering her eyes as if in acknowledgment of his analysis. In a movement guided as much by an unwelcome desire to touch him as it was by a wish to tease, Savannah toyed with the button of his shirt. At once his hand closed over her fingers and he folded her questing hand against his chest.

"I want to know you better," he said. "And I want you to know me. You'll honor your bargain now, won't you, honey?"

She kept her eyes lowered, not quite able to summon the courage it took to meet his intent look while she lied. "Yes," she got out quietly, "I'll pay my debts."

"Thank you, Savannah," he murmured, the dragon's purr in his voice very audible as he kissed her lightly on the forehead. "About your coffee . . ."

"Yes?" she encouraged hesitantly.

"I'm a man of my word." He smiled, taking her hand and leading her toward the kitchen.

Soon she would have to make her bid, Savannah told herself, leaning nonchalantly in the doorway and watching as Cord rummaged in the cupboard for the coffee supplies. He seemed to think she had been totally tamed for the evening and she wondered at his confidence. What an ego Cord must have, Savannah thought admiringly, to believe he had convinced her to spend the weekend with him on the strength of dinner and one kiss. She glanced with seeming idle interest back toward the tiled entry hall and the small chest containing the keys. If she wandered carelessly back out into the living room . . .

"I mean to have a serious talk with you before the weekend is over about your gambling tendencies,"

Cord was saying humorously as he filled the pot with water.

"You don't approve?" she mocked, thinking she rarely played cards and never for money. Perhaps he thought she had a weakness for it. Her arms crossed in front of her, she straightened from her post in the doorframe and wandered casually out into the living room. She paused just within his line of sight and studied a painting of a bullfight.

"I'm not denying it worked to my advantage this evening," he chuckled, "but I must insist you put your evil ways behind you. I wouldn't want another man coming up with the same brainstorm I had!"

"A weekend is an awfully short period of time," Savannah said, barely in sight of the kitchen. "I expect I can swear off gambling for two or three days."

"No one said that this weekend will be the end, Savannah."

"You're beginning to think in terms of a long-range affair?" she taunted lightly. "How exciting. Unless, of course, you're going to prove to be a possessive sort of lover!" She shouldn't have tacked on that last line, Savannah realized. It brought him to the kitchen door where he stood, his large frame outlined by the bright light behind him, watching her. The red of his hair was a fiery brilliance that drew her unwilling attention.

"I shall be a very possessive lover," he confirmed, his voice dangerously soft as his gazed locked on hers. "You lost yourself to me in a game of cards tonight, my little queen, and there's no going back—"

The ringing of the wall phone in the kitchen interrupted the lecture, and Savannah felt an incredible relief as he turned away to answer it. There had been something frightening about his intentness just then, something compelling, as if he really believed he could control her. It had been a silly game of cards, she told herself furiously, realizing she would never have a better chance to walk out than right now.

"Hello?" Cord's rich voice answered the call and Savannah held her breath.

Soundlessly she began edging toward the entry hall, listening to Cord's conversation.

"Look, Ella, I know it's becoming a problem, but I give you my word, I'll take care of everything. Just give me some time—" Whoever he was talking to must have interrupted him at that point because his words broke off sharply.

Savannah had the ring of keys in her hand. With unbelievable care she opened the front door and slipped outside. The Mercedes waited patiently at the curb and she flew down the walk toward it, a sense of exhilaration pouring through her. A moment later she was inside the car, frantically searching for unfamiliar controls. It didn't take long. Very shortly the powerful engine roared to life and Savannah instantly put the car in gear. Thirty seconds later she was halfway down the street, her escape an accomplished fact. She refused to look back.

She had been right about one thing, Savannah told herself the next morning as she boarded the plane for the Monterey Bay area. She did, indeed, regret the previous evening. From start to finish. *My God,* she

63

thought, sinking into a seat and fastening the belt, *what got into me?* It was painfully clear that the minimum loss last night was a good job. She would hand in her resignation as soon as she returned from Carmel—effective immediately! In fact, she decided ruefully, she might even do it by mail. The thought of seeing Cord Harding again in person was violently depressing.

"Coffee?" a hostess inquired politely and Savannah accepted gratefully. She'd had very little sleep the previous night. Not daring to stay at her apartment, she'd left the Mercedes in the security garage with a note inside telling its finder to get the keys from the apartment manager. Then, in a breathless frenzy, half expecting Cord to arrive at any second, she'd loaded her suitcases into her own car, driven to the airport, and spent the remainder of the night in a nearby motel.

She was safe now, Savannah decided. Free to contemplate the disaster that lay behind her. Never had a vacation been more opportunely timed. Two weeks to get over her embarrassment, anger, and self-contempt. She took another sip of her hot coffee and wondered if she could possibly put the blame on the wine. But self-honesty forbade that. The alcohol had undoubtedly fueled the recklessness that had possessed her, but she had been aware of what she was doing all evening. There were no conveniently blank periods in her memory that could be used as an excuse.

The only positive thing to come out of the whole matter was a realization that Jeff Painter no longer seemed in the least important. Savannah sighed, shaking her head regretfully. She had managed to involve herself in such a humiliating situation that all she could think about this morning was a very large redheaded male and her own incredible foolishness. The thought of what Cord's opinion of her must be was no less infuriating than the knowledge that she had deliberately encouraged his opinion by her own abominable behavior. And she had planned to teach him a lesson! Savannah groaned silently to herself, trying to take some comfort from the fact that she had repaid him in some small way for his interference in her life, but it didn't work. The man had simply made a business decision that happened to have impact on her personal life. She'd had no right to blame him for it. There was absolutely no reason to suspect him of malice.

On the other hand, her mind insisted stubbornly, Cord had no right to assume she was fair game last night. He'd deserved being put to the inconvenience of finding his car and having his self-esteem lowered slightly. Hadn't he? The corner of her expressive mouth turned downward in self-disgust. There was no doubt that Cordell Harding was a thoroughly annoying, egotistical male who thought he had only to make a heavy enough pass at a woman to get her. His success and, Savannah admitted honestly, his vital maleness undoubtedly paved an easy way through the byways of sexual liaisons. She should be glad of having had the opportunity to show him that not every woman was waiting to prostrate herself at his feet the moment he declared he wanted her. But it was difficult to look on the bright side when all you could think about was the embarrassment of the whole thing! No, she would never be able to walk back into work two weeks from Monday. She would mail in the resignation. Savannah felt the heat in her cheeks and tried to be grateful for the fact that she was putting a great deal of distance between herself and Costa Mesa. Who said you couldn't run away from your problems?

That last thought cheered her considerably as she collected her baggage at the Monterey airport and rented a car for the short drive to Carmel. Lovely Carmel-by-the-Sea. Quiet, charming, quaint and marvelously relaxing. It was Savannah's favorite vacation spot and she had chosen it this year in preference to Hawaii or Acapulco. True, the nightlife would be a good deal more lively in the other two popular resort areas, but Savannah had opted for a picturesque little inn and the solitude of the Monterey Peninsula beaches. This morning she was especially happy with her choice. The last thing on earth she desired today was the prospect of exciting nightlife! Last night's activities had generated more than enough thrills to last for the next two weeks, she told herself wryly as she parked the car in the tiny lot behind the inn.

"Miss Emery! We've been expecting you," the desk clerk beamed enthusiastically, his cheerful middle-aged face expressing genuine welcome. And a certain amount of male approval, she realized, and then told herself she was being overly sensitive about the looks she was seeing in men's eyes these days.

"We've put you in two nineteen. I hope you'll enjoy it."

"Thank you." Savannah smiled back, glancing contentedly around the cozy lobby with its unabashedly quaint style. "I'm looking forward to this stay," she said, and meant it.

Half an hour later Savannah tugged a pair of snug-fitting designer jeans up the long, shapely length of her legs and slipped her feet into canvas shoes. One of the few advantages of her height, she decided, surveying herself in the mirror, was all that leg! But there were times when she would have traded everything for the feeling of being fragile and petite. She thought wistfully of Jeff's new romance as she donned a bright yellow Windbreaker. What was her name? Alison? Well, Savannah lectured herself grimly, she was no Alison and that was that. Besides, there were other advantages to possessing a certain amount of height and size, she thought with a small grin. Men rarely attempted to take advantage of women who were almost as large as they were! Except men like Cord Harding, she amended ruefully as she made her way downstairs, planning first to return her rented car at the local office and then to head for the antique-shop-lined street that ended in a couple of blocks at the ocean.

On the windswept beach at last, Savannah drew a deep breath and finally began to relax. She set off at a brisk pace along the shoreline, reveling in the sight and sound of the crashing breakers, the gnarled Monterey cypresses clinging precariously to the rocky shore and the expanse of empty beach. She would walk, she decided, until she'd rid herself of the painful memories of last night.

"Excuse me," a male voice interrupted even as Savannah began to fulfill her intentions. "Is this a private walk or would you be willing to share the beach?"

She turned, mildly startled to see a good-looking dark-haired man of about her own age standing on the small cliff above her. Pushing wind-loosened tendrils of jungle-cat brown hair out of her eyes, Savannah smiled politely.

"The beach is free, of course," she said. "I won't chase you off."

"Good." The man grinned cheerfully, clattering down the short incline and walking toward her. Dark eyes flicked over the length of her and Savannah sensed he wasn't displeased with what he'd found. But he was polite about his perusal and she decided not to take umbrage. Something about the dark eyes and the casual California charm of her new acquaintance reminded her of Jeff.

"My name's Eric Daly," he told her hopefully, stopping a few feet away.

"I'm Savannah Emery." She saw his glance go swiftly to her left hand and realized he was looking for signs of a wedding ring. With an aloof smile she started walking again and Eric Daly fell into step alongside.

"Vacationing in Carmel?" he asked chattily, thrusting his hands into his jacket pockets. He was an attractive man and probably knew it, Savannah thought, noting the properly faded color of his tight jeans, the dark hair styled to appear windblown even when he wasn't on a beach, and the expensive velour jacket.

"Yes," she responded a little shortly, not certain she wanted to cultivate the relationship. She'd had enough of men in recent days. A short breather seemed in order. "And you?"

"I'm staying with some friends of mine. They have that house up there on the cliff." He nodded toward an elegant beach home overlooking the ocean. "It's beautiful around here, but a bit on the quiet side. You're here all by yourself?" he added delicately, glancing at her out of the corner of his eye.

"Yes," she retorted coolly. "I came for the peace and quiet." Eric was as tall as Jeff, but not as tall as Cord Harding. Nor did he have Harding's well-muscled build, which was probably Cord's legacy from his days in construction. Still, if she didn't wear heels, Eric would be of a reasonable size for her.

"What's so funny?" Eric demanded warily, seeing the curve of her smile.

"Nothing, really. Just enjoying the day," she said quickly, deliberately letting the smile become the full-blown expression of laughter and warmth that put interview candidates at ease and charmed her friends. It worked its magic once again and Eric grinned back happily. *Probably thinks he's made a conquest,* Savannah sighed inwardly. Men! And then she remembered what Cord had said about her overwhelming a man; how the vast majority would ultimately decide it would be safer to have her for a friend rather than a lover. The remark had annoyed her primarily because she sensed some truth in it. Was Mr. Eric Daly of a similarly weak stripe? Dammit! She was no witch. . . .

"Have you got a car?" Eric asked curiously.

"I turned it in to the rental agency this morning. Decided I wouldn't need one what with having the shops and the ocean and the restaurants all so close to my inn. I'm here to relax," Savannah said with a touch of determination. "I don't plan on doing any driving until I leave."

"Don't you want to take a drive up through the Big Sur country? Or spend some time over in Monterey?" Eric inquired interestedly.

"It's not important. Not this trip."

"Bent on relaxing, are you?" He chuckled. "What do you do for a living that you need so much rest?"

Savannah laughed. "Nothing all that arduous. I'm in personnel work. But the last couple of months have been something of a strain." She shrugged honestly. "How about you?"

"How do I make my living? I'm in real estate. I have a brokerage firm in the San Francisco area."

"With a high-pressure business like that, you must need the vacation even more than I do!" Savannah exclaimed, almost instinctively injecting a note of admiration in her words. It had the usual effect. Eric Daly preened.

"I like the hustle and energy required, but there are times when I need to get away," he acknowledged.

"How long are you staying in Carmel?"

"About a week. You?" He smiled, slanting a speculative glance across at her.

"Two weeks."

"That's a lot of peace and quiet!"

"I need it." She smiled.

They walked and chatted for another hour. Savannah, who never had the least trouble making conversation with anyone, thanks to her training, decided Eric Daly wasn't going to be a source of annoyance after all. In fact he was much more charming than her admirer of last night! When they at last headed back down the beach toward the inn, she didn't make excuses in response to Eric's inevitable question.

"If I promise not to make too much noise and disturb your peace and quiet, would you have dinner with me tonight? I don't know anyone else in town except my friends who own the beach house and they're going to be out for the evening." He smiled invitingly and Savannah could sense his inner confidence that she would accept. But why shouldn't she? He had turned out to be a reasonably intelligent conversationalist and it was flattering to have such an attractive man interested in her after Jeff's defection. One couldn't count Cord Harding's interest, she told herself quickly.

"I'd like that." She nodded immediately, making up her mind.

"Great. There's a nice little place not far from your inn. We can walk. Six thirty okay? We can have a drink before dinner."

"That will be fine." She smiled and watched him leave with curiously mixed emotions. She hadn't come on this trip to make another male acquaintance. In fact, if she had planned it that way, she undoubtedly wouldn't have met anyone! But Eric seemed pleasant and after Cord's cutting comments regarding her handling of the opposite sex, it was soothing to have a male show some interest! With a decisive little nod of her neat head, Savannah climbed the stairs to her room.

Savannah took care with her appearance that evening, perhaps out of some instinctive desire to prove Cord wrong, she admitted to herself wryly. She chose a sleek red dress that clung to her well-proportioned figure and fell to her slender ankles. The scooped neckline showcased the unusual silver pendant she'd found last year while vacationing in Acapulco, and a pair of strappy sandals, chosen for the low heels, completed the outfit. Savannah hardly even noticed the careful selection of low-heeled shoes. It had become the norm for her evening dressing. It was all well and good to be of a stately height when dealing with interview candidates, difficult employees, and management, but there were times when it would have been fun to be cute, tiny, and cuddly! Someone toward whom a man would automatically feel protective. Oh, well, she sighed lightly, one couldn't have everything. She quite firmly refused to think about those moments she had spent dancing in Cord Harding's arms the previous evening.

As usual, Savannah was ready much too early. A bad habit she had tried to break a couple of years ago but had eventually found impossible. She was born to be on time, she thought with a small inner grin, and began rifling through a stack of magazines on the small table near the bed in search of something to read while she waited for Eric. She had just settled down on the seat of an antique armchair and was leafing through a business publication when there was a knock on the door.

She got to her feet, pleased that Eric was turning out to be someone who had the same problem with time as herself. Tossing the magazine down onto the bed, she walked to the door and flung it open with a warm, cheerful smile.

"Hello, Eric," she began before the door was completely open. "I'm glad you're not one of those men who assumes a woman is always going to be late—"

Savannah's words were cut off in thunderstruck amazement as she stared for a split second at the apparition outside her door. The tawny gold eyes opened wide in horror and she swallowed in disbelief.

"No!" she yelped in dismay and did the first thing that crossed her mind. She slammed the door at once and locked it. An instant later she sagged against the wood and stared blankly across the room. It couldn't be! Cord Harding couldn't be standing out there not more than two feet away.

But the patient knock came again.

"I'm afraid it really is me," Cord called gently through the door, his low rumble of a voice carrying clearly.

Stepping away from the door as if it had suddenly become superheated metal, Savannah turned and gazed at it, transfixed. She must be imagining things! Surely Cord Harding wouldn't have followed her all the way to Carmel for—for *revenge!*

"You might as well open the door, Savannah," he said calmly. "I'm not going to go away."

"You *have* to go away!" she managed to declare with fine illogic, her eyes on the door handle as if Cord would somehow turn it and walk into the room. But that was ridiculous. He couldn't melt locks!

"Let me in, Savannah," he ordered coolly.

"What will you do if I don't?" she challenged wildly, chewing on her knuckles in a childish gesture she hadn't used in years, "Break down the door? Even you wouldn't make that sort of scene!"

"Of course not," he agreed, sounding amused. "Why should I go to that trouble when all I have to do is walk downstairs and get a key?"

"Cord, please! Go away!" she begged, feeling quite desperate.

"I can't do that, Savannah," he murmured almost apologetically through the door. "There are too many things we have to settle between us."

"Like what?" she demanded furiously. "There's nothing for us to talk about and you know it!"

"How about the little matter of the right rear fender on the Mercedes?" he suggested.

"The Mercedes!" she gasped, stunned. "I didn't hurt it! It was fine when I left it in the garage!" Visions of an exorbitant foreign-car repair bill danced in her head, and with a grim feeling of inevitable disaster Savannah put a hand on the door knob.

74

With vast reluctance she slid aside the lock and slowly twisted the handle, squeezing her wide eyes shut for an instant before she risked peeking around the edge.

Through the two-inch gap between wall and door Savannah stared up at her unwelcome visitor. Cord returned the fascinated look with one of patient humor. The gray-green eyes gleamed down at her as he put a large hand solidly against the door and pushed.

"The car isn't the only matter we need to discuss," he observed, forcing the door slowly open. "Who is Eric?"

CHAPTER FOUR

"Eric," Savannah repeated blankly, all thought of the younger man having flown from her mind the moment she absorbed the impact of Cord at the door. Memory returned in a rush. "Eric!" she said again with sudden conviction, even as she backed helplessly toward the middle of the room.

"Yes, Eric," he mimicked reproachfully, kicking the door shut with a careless action and beginning to advance toward her. One heavy russet brow lifted admonishingly. "Don't tell me you've not only deprived me of my winnings, you're also intending to give them away to another man!"

Savannah felt herself turning a shade of red that almost matched her dress. She made a desperate bid to recover her self-control. The first step, common sense dictated, was to stop physically retreating. Very bad body language, she told herself forcefully.

It gave Cord the notion he somehow held an advantage.

"I don't know what you think you're going to accomplish, Cord," she began staunchly, halting her backward progress and drawing herself to her full height. With most men that would have been quite effective. Unfortunately Harding was not most men.

"Yes, you do," he contradicted easily, green eyes lighting as they swept her from head to foot. "I'm here to collect my payment." He came to a halt about three feet away and simply smiled at her. Savannah decided she could trust that smile about as far as she could the leer of a tiger.

"Don't be ridiculous," she said tightly, trying for a suitably lofty approach. What a ghastly situation! And Eric would be arriving at any moment! "You have absolutely no right to hold me to that—that idiotic bet and you know it! It was made under duress, for heaven's sake!"

"I didn't force you to gamble away an entire weekend of your life," he pointed out virtuously and with the air of a man who knows he's in the right. He glanced around the quaint little room with an approving nod. "A charming inn, by the way. This will be a delightful place to collect the debt you owe me. You still have to deliver an evening to compensate for the Friday night you deprived me of when you ran off. Perhaps I'll stay over on Monday night so you can make up for it."

"Will you stop behaving as if there were something normal about all this?" Savannah glared furiously. "I'm not responsible for what happened last night. You—you encouraged me! Egged me on! I have no intention of— Get out of that chair," she choked, outraged as Cord lowered his lean frame onto the room's one seat.

"I want to be comfortable while I listen to the excuses," he explained politely, meeting her flashing gold eyes with an innocent expression that thoroughly alarmed Savannah.

"What game are you playing, Cord?" she demanded heatedly, facing him with her hands on her hips.

"I stopped playing games last night," he retorted evenly, the fingers of one hand tapping the arm of the chair in a manner that reminded her of a large cat flicking its tail before it pounced. "You're the one who's continuing to indulge yourself in games of chance."

"You can't really expect me to pay a gambling debt like the one you led me into making last night. You must have known when I walked out the front door—"

"Taking my car with you," he interjected.

"*Borrowing* your car," she corrected immediately, aware of another wave of embarrassment over the incident. "You must have realized then that I had no intention of going through with the deal!"

"I realized you had gotten cold feet at the last minute," he began soothingly, a superior sort of smile curving his hard mouth as he watched her.

"I never intended to go through with it! At the moment I made the bet I told myself I wouldn't pay it!" she exclaimed. "It was not a question of chickening out at the last minute, you abominable man!"

"Had your fingers crossed behind your back, did you?" he inquired coolly, the amusement in his eyes growing. "Well, in that case this is as good a time as any to teach you about the sanctity of gambling debts."

"Cord, listen to me," Savannah bit out savagely. "I don't have time to talk about this now. I've got a friend arriving at any moment and I want you out of here!"

"Ah, yes. The Eric person. We do have a lot to discuss, don't we, Savannah? Why don't you sit down and stop pacing back and forth like that? You'll wear yourself out."

"This is my room, dammit! If I want to exhaust myself pacing the floor, I will!"

"That's what I like in a woman," Cord remarked dryly. "A touch of spirit."

"Are you going to remove yourself?" she asked tautly, turning to glare at him over her shoulder as she halted by the window.

"Come now, sweetheart," he growled softly. "You can't expect me to simply walk off and give my prize to another man. Didn't I tell you last night I tend to be possessive? And I'm sure any of my business associates will vouch for my tenacity."

"You don't own me!" she managed, beginning to get a little frightened. He looked so big, so immovable sitting there.

"I own two nights and two days of your life," he reminded her.

Savannah flinched at the cold-blooded way he said it. Everything had seemed so simple last night! "You know I was only using you to work off some of my frustration over Jeff Painter," she began, wondering if a more apologetic tactic might be effective. "I'd had a little too much to drink, I suppose, and I couldn't help but blame you for having been the reason Jeff had gone to San Diego in the first place. I know that wasn't logical," she admitted at once, slanting a glance at him out of the corner of her eye to see how her humble tone was going down. "I mean, I'm aware that the transfer was strictly a business matter. But it was embarrassing for me last night and I wanted a bit of revenge. Can't you understand that? You're the one who suggested I use the card game to get even with you!"

"I understand. I did last night."

"Then why are you hounding me?" she demanded, whirling away from the window to confront him from across the room. "If it's the car you're worried about, I'll be glad to give you the name of my insurance company—"

"I'd rather take the payment out of your soft hide, my sweet Savannah," Cord chuckled.

She blinked, startled. "What are you talking about?"

"I'm talking about making love to you until you go all soft and wild in my arms." He was on his feet now, coming toward her as he spoke. The deep voice had dropped to a husky, sexy register that sent tremors of nervous response along Savannah's nerve endings. "I'm talking about making you deliver on the promises you made with those golden eyes. I'm talking about a whole weekend of seeing you smile just for me. . . ."

Savannah stared at him, uncertain of his intentions and half paralyzed by the sheer male intent in his words. "Cord, be reasonable," she whispered falteringly. "You can't force me—"

"Who said anything about forcing you?" he asked, standing very close but not touching her. "I've done a lot of thinking about the best way to handle you, my little gambler."

"You have?" she asked warily, not liking the gleam in the gray-green eyes.

"Umm. Want to hear my analysis of the situation and my final decision on how best to collect from you?" he inquired helpfully.

Savannah watched him cautiously, assessing his mood. She couldn't fully understand this whimsical touch in him. What was he up to? He didn't seem about to use force though, and that gave her a measure of courage.

"Some other time," she told him promptly, striving to regain some control of the scene. She put a firm hand on his sleeve and tried to propel him toward the door. She might as well have been trying to push a large boulder. "I want you to leave, Cord."

"Not yet," he responded, glancing idly down at her hand on his arm. Then he raised his hands, planting the palms against the wall behind her and trapping Savannah between his arms. "First I think I deserve a proper welcoming kiss after having traveled all this way to claim my winnings. . . ."

"No!" Savannah twisted away as Cord lowered his

head but one large hand left the wall long enough to catch her chin rather firmly and hold her steady.

"Yes," he countered, his breath warm on her cheek just before his mouth covered hers with a kind of lazy, toying deliberation. Savannah felt his other arm go around her, tightening until she couldn't move. It was last night all over again, she thought, panicked.

Desperately she attempted to free her hands, fold them into fists and use them against the broad muscled chest, but he caught first one and then the other, clamping them in the vise of his own hand and holding them behind her back. He never hurt her in the process but there was a dismaying sensation of solidity in the grip.

"Stop it," Savannah heard herself beg, even as her mouth began to soften in response to his insistence. What in the world was wrong with her that this man could command such a reaction from her? She didn't even like him!

"Don't worry," he gritted heavily against her lips. "I'm just taking a little on account."

Savannah was aware of being gently crowded against the wall until she was caught between its unforgiving surface and Cord's equally unyielding frame.

"I don't owe you anything," she wailed in a combination of anger and frustration at her growing feeling of helplessness.

"You owe me everything of yourself, don't you realize that yet?" he demanded in his dragon's purr as he nuzzled the tip of her ear. "I'm here to collect.

But you needn't panic, little amazon. Unlike you, I keep my word and last night I promised not to rush you." He released her wrists to frame her upturned face with strong, probing fingers. "I'll give you time. . . ."

"How much?" she asked instantly, seeing her one possibility.

He shrugged. "A couple of days, perhaps. I can take some time off from the office. . . ."

"A couple of days!" she almost shrieked in exasperation. "That's hardly long enough to convince someone to have an affair!"

"Why not?" he asked reasonably, the corner of his firm mouth quirking upward in mild amusement. "It's not as if we're starting from scratch as two perfect strangers. We already know how things are going to end. You won't deny me my just reward, will you, my sweet Savannah?" he finished persuasively.

"With the greatest pleasure!" Savannah flattened her hands against his shoulders and shoved, but it was hopeless. And all these years she'd been under the illusion that she wanted a big, strong man who could make her feel weak and feminine! What an idiot she had been! She would have given anything right now for Cord to be much smaller and far more manageable.

"Lucky for you I took an oath of patience before I bought my ticket on the airplane this morning," he mocked lightly.

"Cord, please," she tried desperately. "I have a date tonight and he'll be along any minute. Can't you understand? I don't want to have to explain your presence."

"Where did you meet the mysterious Eric?" Cord asked pleasantly, still holding her within the circle of his arms.

"On the beach today," she explained impatiently. "He's staying with some friends in the area and he invited me out to dinner. It will be very embarrassing trying to explain you. Surely you can see that."

"Do you want me to do the explaining?" he suggested cheerfully.

"No!"

"Well, you'll just have to tell him to go away, then."

"I will not tell him to go away! He's a very nice person who's invited me to dinner and I have no intention of humiliating myself by telling him I can't go out with him because my boss has ordered me not to!" Savannah grated furiously.

A loud knock on the heavy door interrupted Savannah's angry speech. She froze, her eyes locking onto Cord's gray-green ones in wide dismay.

"That's Eric," she whispered frantically.

"So?" he asked in a low, persuasive tone. "Tell him to leave."

"I can't do that!" she shot back in soft defiance as she struggled to disengage herself. "I have a date with him tonight and I'm going to keep it. If you're any sort of gentleman, you'll get into that closet and hide!"

"Hide?" he asked in astonishment, although he was kind enough to keep his voice down. "In the closet? Are you crazy? This is my weekend, not Eric's!"

The knock sounded again.

"I'll be right there, Eric," Savannah called hastily. "I'm on the phone.

"Take your time," the other man responded obligingly. "I'll wait out here."

"Well?" Savannah hissed, glowering up at Cord. "Are you going to embarrass me or are you going to do the polite thing and disappear?" It was hopeless, of course. Savannah knew it. Cord was going to make a scene and humiliate her even more than he had already. But she had to make one more appeal.

For a long suspenseful moment Cord watched her as if trying to decide on a plan of action. "I swore I'd be patient with you," he finally said slowly, "but I'm not particularly inclined to start hiding in closets so you can play your games with other men. That sort of thing tries a man's patience a little too far, don't you think?"

There was laughter in his eyes and Savannah wanted to slap him. "Please?" she tried softly, opening her eyes in wide supplication. It didn't take much effort.

"The last time I gave in to your pleading I wound up with an empty bed and a scarred Mercedes."

"Cord, if you'll just grant me this one request, I swear I'll return after the evening is over and talk the whole thing out with you."

"Word of honor?" he mocked.

"Yes."

"No running off into the night, leaving me to wait forever in a closet?"

"Cord! For heaven's sake!"

"When will you be back?" he murmured.

"I don't know exactly. But we won't be late," she added quickly, seeing his expression harden. "I'll—I'll tell Eric I want to return early." She waited tensely, beginning to experience a ray of hope.

"Okay," Cord said finally, turning abruptly and stalking past her. "But if you don't mind, I'll hide in the bathroom instead of the closet. I'm not sure I'd fit."

Savannah stared after him, stunned. He was going to do it! He was going to keep out of sight while she left with Eric. She couldn't absorb it!

"Th—thank you," she breathed, not quite daring to believe she'd won so easily. What was going on here?

"Think nothing of it," he counseled, stepping into the bathroom and turning to face her, his hand on the door. "Just make sure you're back here by ten."

"Ten! No one gets in by ten! I haven't been in by ten since I was in high school!"

"Take your choice," he offered laconically. "Be back here by ten or I'll undertake to explain the entire situation to your Eric."

"I'll be back," she promised hastily, unwilling to lose the advantage she had so unexpectedly gained.

"Good. My decision to be patient is certainly going to be put to the test tonight. Already I'm feeling like a complete fool."

"I'm very grateful," Savannah began, reaching out

to pull the door to the bathroom shut. In another moment she would be free!

"Just remember, Savannah," Cord said, his grasp on the door keeping it from closing. "Ten o'clock."

"I'll remember," she vowed, thinking that if she ever got out of the room tonight she might never return!

"Five minutes after the magic hour and I'll come looking. It's a small town, Savannah."

Savannah sighed in resignation, realizing she really was going to have to return and have it out with him. She couldn't have him following her around like this forever!

"I'll be back."

"Yes, I know you will," he smiled kindly and allowed her to shut the door.

Savannah took a deep breath, snatched up her shawl, and hastened across the room.

"Eric, I'm terribly sorry to keep you waiting," she said quickly as she hurried out into the hall where he was standing. She was incredibly glad Cord had actually consented to hide in the bathroom. Once the door was open even a small way, it provided a clear view into the small room. She didn't stop to question Cord's amazing cooperation.

"No problem. Finish your conversation? I didn't mean to rush you," Eric said politely, adjusting the lacy shawl over her shoulders, his eyes clearly enjoying the sight of her.

"Oh, yes. A—a friend from the office," Savannah lied quickly. "She was calling to say she was trying to make it to Carmel herself while I was staying here."

"Great! If she shows up, I'll find a friend and we can all double."

Savannah glanced up apprehensively into Eric's enthusiastic face. That was the problem with little white lies. They tended to snowball on one.

"I think you're going to like this restaurant," Eric went on a few minutes later as they stepped out onto the sidewalk. "It's only a couple of blocks from here. Specializes in French cooking with fish and it has an excellent wine list."

"It sounds marvelous," Savannah agreed, trying to hide a nervous glance upward to the second floor of the inn. A second later she wished she'd avoided the temptation. Cord was there, watching them from her window. As soon as he saw her looking up at him he smiled benignly and waved in a cheerful fashion. But it didn't fool Savannah for one instant. She'd seen the hardness in his face before he'd replaced it with that false politeness and it had made her shiver. She found herself suddenly wondering why he had let her go out with Eric. The action didn't fit the expression in those narrowed green eyes.

Once again Savannah had cause to be grateful for her personnel background. Years of having to deal with a wide spectrum of human nature had made the business of carrying on a conversation under less than perfect conditions an innate skill. But even as she discussed the menu with Eric and applauded his choice in wine, her mind churned over the question of how to deal with Cord Harding. What in the world was she going to do with him? How long did he mean to keep following her around the countryside, waiting for his "payment"? The entire matter was horribly unsettling!

"You sound as if you enjoy the real estate business," she remarked at one point to Eric as she toyed with her salad. Her appetite was normally quite healthy, but tonight . . .

"I was lucky enough to cash in on some of the California boom," he chuckled in self-satisfaction. "Real estate is one of the last frontiers for the entrepreneur. A business where one can still build a fortune."

"I'm afraid I've rather locked myself into the old nine-to-five routine," Savannah admitted with an apologetic smile.

"You could take your skills and sell them independently, I'll bet. You know, some kind of consulting work, perhaps?" Eric suggested helpfully, leaning forward to make his point.

Savannah glanced up to respond to his remark and froze. Over Eric's shoulder she saw the maitre d' guiding a lone diner toward a window table set for one. Cord! He'd followed her to the restaurant!

"What's the matter, Savannah? Are you all right?" Eric inquired, sounding genuinely worried. She realized that her feeling of having gone white was probably based on fact.

"I'm fine," she reassured him gamely, reaching for her glass of wine and consuming a fortifying gulp. Out of the corner of her eye she could see Cord watching her as he picked up his menu. She realized he was smiling in what was undoubtedly meant to be a polite, breezy fashion. But his smiles always reminded her of the grin of a wild creature when it sights its prey, and this one was no different. What was he going to do? She sneaked a peek at the watch on her wrist. Only seven o'clock. It wasn't anywhere near the hour when her whole world would turn into a pumpkin!

"Have you done any real estate investing yourself?" Eric rambled on, returning to his favorite topic. "Do you own your own home?"

"I'm afraid not," she managed, terribly aware of Cord's intent regard.

"What are you doing with your money?" Eric demanded, clearly about to jump into the role of wise financial counselor. Savannah was in no mood to be treated to a monologue on how to handle her money. She had other problems tonight.

"I'm in the stock market," she explained, hoping that would put a halt to the trend of the conversation.

"The market!" he exclaimed disapprovingly. "That's no place for a woman!"

Savannah raised one eyebrow coolly. "On the contrary." She smiled dangerously. "It has the same lure for me as real estate has for you. An entrepreneurial frontier. There are a lot of women in this country who invest in securities."

"It's entirely the wrong approach," Eric proclaimed, failing completely to pick up on Savannah's unwillingness to play the role of helpless female in need of male financial advice. "What you need is to get started in a sound piece of real estate . . ." he began pompously.

"I don't happen to be interested in that type of investing," she said sweetly, trying to cut off the discussion once more. Cord's smile had broadened slightly. Had he sensed her growing impatience with Eric? She tried to fix her dinner partner with a warm look that might belie her irritation.

"It's probably a question of responsibility, isn't it?" Eric asked with an air of superiority. "You undoubtedly don't like the thought of having to deal with all the details of real estate, managing tenants, finding buyers, handling agents."

"Let's just say I find the market much more exciting," she retorted dryly. "Cheap thrills!"

"You shouldn't be flippant about it. It's your whole future we're discussing," Eric instructed, pointing his fork at her for emphasis.

"If you don't mind," Savannah stated deliberately, wishing Cord would stop watching her with that expectant look, "I'd rather not discuss my future tonight."

Eric hesitated, obviously torn between the desire to set her feet on the path of fiscal righteousness and the wish to pursue the romantic side of the evening. "Some other time perhaps," he finally agreed, smiling across at her with a look that said he understood she probably didn't want to burden her feminine brain with such weighty matters this evening.

"Perhaps," Savannah compromised wryly, knowing full well she had no intention of renewing the subject.

The tension that had filled the dining room the moment Cord had entered seemed to thicken as the evening wore on. Savannah felt it in every square inch of her body, felt it tightening every nerve as ten o'clock drew closer and closer. She was going to have to get rid of Eric and have the matter out with Cord. That was all there was to it. Better to face it and get the unpleasant scene over with than put up with the never-ending fear of having an unwelcome red-headed shadow on future dates! She would just have to be very, very firm with Cordell Harding, Savannah told herself as Eric paid the dinner bill and guided her out of the restaurant.

"What about an after-dinner drink in that little place next to your inn?" Eric suggested, wholly unaware of the turmoil Savannah was experiencing. "They've got a small combo playing, I believe."

Savannah glanced at her watch. "Oh, Eric, I'd really love to, but some other time perhaps. I hate to be a poor sport, but I'm afraid I'm rather exhausted. Didn't get much sleep last night and it's been a hard week. Would you be offended if I suggested we call it an evening?" She fixed him with her best tawny-eyed appeal and a warm smile.

"So early?" he began, appearing somewhat startled. He probably wasn't accustomed to having his dates want to go home early.

"I hadn't expected to be asked out at all this evening," she explained ruefully. "My original plans included being sound asleep by now!"

"I see." He hesitated. "Just one drink?"

"Well . . ." She finally gave in and nodded. She still had half an hour.

But there was no peace to be found in the small nightclub. Eric had no sooner ordered the drinks than Savannah felt the prickles along her spine and knew Cord was in the room. A moment later she spotted him through the smoky darkness, leaning casually against the bar, a glass in his hand. He was watching her again, and when he caught her eye, he flicked a pointed glance down at his watch.

Savannah gritted her teeth and considered a variety of actions, all of which would have both stunned and embarrassed poor Eric. She couldn't do that to the younger man, she decided grimly, and set herself to the business of trying to be pleasant for another twenty minutes. The only satisfaction she got out of the remainder of her date was when Eric unknowingly led her past Cord's lean figure on the way out of the lounge. For a second Cord was so close, he could have reached out and touched her, and Savannah saw the wicked laughter in the gleaming green depths of his eyes. Very deliberately she bared her even white teeth and took a step that brought the short heel of her sandal down on the Italian leather toe of one large shoe.

"Oh, excuse me," she breathed in the quick, apologetic tones one uses with a stranger one has bumped into accidentally.

"Think nothing of it," he retorted silkily, adding just under his breath as she swept on past, "I'll put it on your tab."

* * *

94

At least the corridor outside her room was empty, Savannah thought in relief as Eric reluctantly stopped at her door. With any luck at all, Cord would have the decency to remain out of sight while she said her good-night.

"I sure hate to call it an evening so early," Eric said with a trace of huskiness in his voice as he held her hand and smiled charmingly into her eyes. He was going to kiss her, Savannah realized a little nervously and then wondered at her own reaction. After all, she should be flattered that this good-looking, successful man had found her attractive. Especially when she hadn't exactly been at her most amusing on the first date! So why this slightly furtive feeling, as if it were somehow wrong to let Eric kiss her?

"I had a lovely time," she assured him, as much to convince herself as Eric. "I'm very sorry about this, but I'm afraid I do need some rest." She smiled apologetically.

"I'll call you tomorrow," he murmured, bending close.

Savannah was obligingly lifting her face for his kiss, her eyes closing in the approved fashion, when Eric, apparently jostled from behind, suddenly lost his balance and almost fell against her.

"What the hell . . . !" he began, turning to glare at the large man who had unexpectedly emerged from the stairway.

"I beg your pardon," Cord said smoothly, his focus on Savannah's frowning features. "Must have stumbled coming around the corner." He made a polite show of straightening Eric's coat and then began fishing around in his own pockets. "Damn, I know I put those keys in my jacket before I left this evening," he muttered half to himself. "You two staying here?" he went on conversationally, speaking to Eric and Savannah impartially.

"Savannah is. I'm staying with friends in town," Eric explained a bit grumpily, beginning to realize that Cord wasn't going to quickly disappear into a nearby room.

"Great place, isn't it?" Cord remarked to Savannah, who smiled back very thinly. "Can't wait to get down to the beach tomorrow. And I hear they have an excellent brunch on Sundays. I expect you enjoy all the antique and art shops, don't you? Women always seem to like that sort of thing," he explained kindly to Eric. "Actually, I'm going to do a little looking in the art line, myself. I could use something for the mantel over my fireplace. Don't suppose you've had a chance to see anything appropriate yet, have you?"

"Er—no, I'm afraid not." Eric looked helplessly at a silently seething Savannah. "I guess I'll be on my way. . . ."

"Thanks again," she said politely, wishing she could yell at Cord instead. "I'll be expecting your call in the morning."

"Yes, well, good night, then." With a last, frustrated glance at Cord, Eric took himself off, leaving a furious Savannah behind.

"That," she declared violently as Eric disappeared, "was entirely unnecessary."

96

"What do you mean, unnecessary? You were going to let him kiss you!"

"So what? It was none of your business!" she stormed, digging out her key and fitting it into the lock with a savage motion.

"The hell it wasn't! This was supposed to be my weekend! I let him have dinner with you, didn't I? How much more do you expect from me?"

Savannah ignored him, marching forward into her room and switching on the light.

"Besides," Cord announced as if it were the last word, "he's just another Jeff Painter."

"I happen to like the Jeff Painter type!"

"No, you don't," he contradicted easily, once again taking the only chair in the room. "At least you won't after you've learned to appreciate my various and assorted qualities instead!" He stretched out his legs and surveyed one shoe. "That was a nasty blow you landed there in the nightclub," he noted casually.

Savannah heard the contentment in his voice and realized Cord was quite satisfied with the way things were progressing, as if he could afford a certain amount of banter because ultimately he knew he was in control. That confidence worried her but she refused to reveal it as she removed her shawl and unfastened the necklace she had worn. "You had a good deal more coming to you than a crushed toe," she bit out, watching his face in the mirror.

"Lucky for you I've decided to teach you how to be a good loser." Cord sat in a totally relaxed position, watching her small actions at the dressing table with undisguised interest.

Her dark brows drawing together in a severe frown, Savannah turned away to sink down onto the bed, facing him. She deliberately left her hair coiled regally in place. Something about that look in his eyes told her he was hoping she would remove a few more of the trappings of the evening. Probably thought that if she got comfortable enough, she would be more vulnerable, Savannah decided grimly.

"All right, Cord," she began in a deliberately remote and cool tone, "let's get this over. It's clear that because I ran out on you last night—"

"In the middle of a conversation with a very dear aunt, I might add," he injected.

"I realize my departure has ruffled your male ego. I've become some sort of challenge to you, haven't I?" Not waiting for him to answer, Savannah plowed on. "I know I'm a far cry from your usual type of girl friend. Office gossip is quite certain you prefer small, decorative blondes, so there's no point trying to make me think I'm anything more than a passing novelty." She took a deep breath. "I'm sorry about what happened last night. I honestly don't know what got into me, but I can guarantee you that gambling, let alone gambling for those kinds of stakes, is not routine for me! I'm also very sorry if your car was scratched while it was in the apartment-house garage. I will, of course, pay for it. As for the rest, I would be very appreciative if you would simply forget my idiotic behavior at the party." There! She had made a full apology. What more could she do?

"Very nicely said," he approved in a low growl, the green eyes never leaving her carefully composed features. "There's just one small problem."

"What's that?" she demanded tightly, sensing his determination and wanting to run from it.

"I'm not prepared to give up what I won last night," he murmured. "I want you."

CHAPTER FIVE

"Well, you can't have me," Savannah gasped, stunned by the outrageous simplicity of his words. She attempted to cover her nervousness with a haughty tilt of her head, disdaining to meet his eyes.

"Shall I tell you exactly how I mean to go about convincing you to pay your gambling debts?" He grinned engagingly. "I know where I went wrong last night, you see."

"There's nothing you can do!"

"Oh, yes, there is. I'm going to haunt you," he explained, eyes gleaming in anticipation and laughter. "Just as I did tonight. You won't be able to go anywhere with another man without me being right behind you."

"You can't do that!" she snarled, infuriated. She leaped from the bed and paced distractedly to the window, turning her back on him. "That constitutes harassment or something. I'm sure it's against the law! I won't have it!"

"Then you'd better make up your mind to give me my weekend," he retorted. The amusement was still plain in his voice, but now there was a touch of iron. Savannah flinched slightly. She knew enough about Cord Harding to know he almost never deviated from a goal.

"I won't allow you to force me into this!" she breathed.

"Ah, but that's the beauty of my plan. There's no force involved. Hopefully."

"What do you mean?" she grated, realizing some part of her was actually intrigued. What was going on in that conniving brain of his?

"It means that I'm basing the success of the plans on my ability to hang on to my patience," he admitted ruefully. "A weak point, I'm afraid. Still," he added, brightening, "I'm going to try."

"You think I'm going to get so sick and tired of having you follow me around on dates that I'll pay you off just to get rid of you?" Savannah kept her gaze on the cluster of cypress trees visible through the window. If he wasn't going to threaten her with force, there were possibilities . . .

"I'm counting on creating a conditioned response in you," he chuckled wickedly. "Every time you return from a date with another man, you're going to find yourself saying good night in my arms, not his. After a while you'll simply accept the inevitable."

"You're crazy!" she gulped, having visions of an endless future of Jeff Painters and Eric Dalys being

102

jostled and chased off when they brought her home at the end of an evening. It was ludicrous! What's more it wouldn't work!

"I don't think it will take too long. You strike me as a fast learner," he said bracingly.

"I'll be quitting my job when I return to Costa Mesa, and if you persist in hounding me, I'll simply move into another apartment! You'll never find me!" she threatened, swinging around to glare at him.

"Yes, I will," he stated with supreme assurance. Savannah believed him! "But I don't think it will come to that," he went on reflectively. "I told you I know where I went wrong last night. . . ."

"Got it all figured out, have you?" she snapped, lifting her chin.

"I think so. The problem last night was that you couldn't handle the inevitability of the whole matter. By the terms of the wager, I had set the time and the place of your surrender and that was more than your pride could swallow. I can understand that," he said sympathetically, smiling straight at her in a way that heightened Savannah's inner tension. "Under my new approach the inevitability is still present, but you will more or less set the time and place."

"Is that it?" she muttered scathingly, unable to believe what she was hearing. "Well, let me tell you something, that's not even the beginning! You've left out a few other influencing factors such as love and friendship and an emotional commitment on both our parts and all the other things that go into a relationship! Can't you understand, Cord Harding? I wouldn't spend a weekend with you unless we were so much in love that nothing else mattered! Do you know what I'm talking about? Or can you only view women as potential conquests? Temporary *weekend* amusements? I was a novelty for you last night, and when I walked out, I somehow graduated to the status of challenge. Your male ego took a beating and you've convinced yourself you have to collect the wager in order to salve your stupid pride!"

"You," he suddenly growled, green eyes narrowing, "know nothing about my motives so don't try second-guessing them!" He was out of the chair and reaching for her before Savannah could sidestep. Strong hands closed around her waist and she was yanked against the tough, hard length of him in an instant, left to wonder what had happened to the almost whimsical humor that had been in his eyes only seconds ago.

"I, on the other hand," he went on deliberately, studying her wide-eyed expression with a certain satisfaction, "understand you completely. You're a lot like me, Savannah Emery, and if you hadn't been so wrapped up trying to seduce Jeff Painter during the past two months, you'd have seen that!"

"That's not true!" she gulped, trying to reassert a measure of control over the situation. "You and I have nothing in common! And I was not trying to seduce Jeff!" she yelped belatedly, incensed.

"Yes, you were." Cord grinned, the laughter back in his eyes. "Why don't you try seducing me instead? I won't run off and find a safer, nonthreatening female as he did."

Before she quite realized what she was doing,

Savannah swung her palm in an arc that ended smartly against the side of his face. In the timeless moment of charged silence that followed she knew a wave of shock so overpowering that it blanked out the painful stinging of her hand. Never had she done anything like that! And from the flash of startled anger in Cord's face, he was not accustomed to such action either. But his hold on her waist never slackened, and Savannah realized there was no way to escape retribution if he chose to administer it. Very bravely she met the darkening green of his gaze and stood quite still in the hard circle of his arms.

"You do try a man's patience," he said at last in an even, laconic tone.

"You—you had that coming," she managed between trembling lips. "You were insulting me. . . ."

"No, I wasn't, but we'll skip the argument for now. Just be grateful, my sweet amazon, that I've already made a decision not to use force. You might keep in mind, however, that all decisions are revocable by the one who makes them! It wouldn't do to push me too far."

He wasn't going to retaliate. Savannah could sense it quite clearly, and the knowledge brought back her courage. For the moment she didn't stop to question his forbearance but rushed to find out how deep it went.

"This decision of yours," she taunted, slanting a speculative glance up into his set face. "Exactly what are its limits? Are you guaranteeing not to go beyond the nuisance stage?"

He took a deep breath before answering. "I have no wish to force you into my bed. I want you there because you want the same thing."

She nodded. "A matter of pride, is it? Your ego doesn't care for the notion that you can't persuade a woman to have a weekend affair with you without resorting to force." A touch of complacence replaced some of her earlier nervousness. If Cord was going to be all talk and no dangerous action, she might be able to deal with him yet.

"I'm hoping the—er—nuisance value alone will suffice," he retorted dryly, undoubtedly aware of her quickly resurfacing self-confidence.

"No force?" she pressed, her fingertips drumming softly on his jacket sleeve.

"No force," he confirmed. "I'll even let you be the one to call a halt to our lovemaking," he added magnanimously.

"If I'm in charge, there won't be any lovemaking to halt!" she snapped back.

"Well," he hedged a little ruefully, "I'm afraid I can't surrender all my male prerogatives." The corner of his mouth lifted slightly. "There will be times, such as now, when the need to demonstrate that you're not invulnerable to me will be almost overpowering!" Too late Savannah realized his intention and tried to twist aside, but Cord's easy strength held her still for his kiss, and even as she fought it she sensed that this was where the real menace in him lay.

"Remember," he whispered huskily as his mouth traced the line of her jaw up to her ear, "I'll let you

106

stop me eventually. You have nothing to fear from me so why not let yourself go? Think how much pleasure you'll have later when you send me away unsatisfied. You'll be able to lead me on, make me think you're succumbing, and then send me off to a cold shower. . . ." There was a persuasive, coaxing edge to his words that seemed to reach right into her bones.

"And you'll go?" she gritted, steeling herself against the sensuous assault. He made her feel so small and fragile when he held her like this!

"Oh, yes, I'll go," he promised. "If you send me away at the last moment, I'll leave. But for now why don't you show me some of that fire I've seen waiting to explode and engulf a man?" His hand moved up to grasp the nape of her neck and then his fingers were in the sleekly coiled knot of hair, loosening the dark strands until the pins fell to the rug. With a sigh of male delight, Cord roped the thickness of the curving waves around his fingers, using it to hold her in place for the plundering of his mouth.

Savannah felt the languid sensation she had known last night and tried to tell herself not to let it overcome her. But the temptation was so strong! In a sense he had offered to let her play with fire, promising not to let her get burned. If he meant what he said, if he really would leave when she denied him the final surrender . . .

"That's it," he muttered thickly, feeling her relax against him. "Take some pleasure and then have some revenge. What more could you ask for?"

"I'm capable of doing my own rationalizing!" she managed to say and heard him give a low laugh.

"But you see how well I can do it for you? That's because we're so much alike, you and I," he told her, one hand exploring the curve of her hip before it began working its way up to the top of her zipper.

"No," she protested faintly, her fingers digging fiercely into the muscles of his neck as she felt the zipper beginning to open.

"Don't worry. I won't forget my promise. Oh, my sweet, fiery Savannah, you go to my head, do you realize that?" he grated as he touched the soft warm skin of her back. "I want to know the passion you promise a man with those eyes. And with me you won't have to hold back," he vowed, easing the front of her dress forward until she stood in his arms wearing only the lacy white bra above her waist.

Savannah closed her eyes, knowing it was a futile attempt to ignore his relentless attack. When she felt him unclasp the bra, she moaned softly and buried her face against his shoulder. His hands cupped her breasts and he used his thumbs to tease the pink tips until the nipples hardened in desire.

"Cord," she got out in a small cry that sounded like the meowing of a kitten.

"Not yet," he told her, letting her feel the disturbing, entirely masculine need in him. He shifted his weight, pulling her hips tightly against his own. "You see how vulnerable I am to you, sweetheart?" he whispered encouragingly.

With a swift movement that left her momentarily disoriented, Cord slipped the red dress down to her ankles, lifted her free of the folds, and carried her the few feet to the bed. He set her down gently on the covers, his eyes never leaving her half-closed ones as he shrugged out of his jacket, unbuttoned and peeled off the white shirt. Then he threw himself down beside her, putting out a hand to gather her close.

"You're perfect for my bed," he smiled in satisfaction, running his hands in delight over the length of her body, which was now covered only by panties.

"This—this is my bed, not yours!" she heard herself say, even as she shivered in response to his possessive touch.

"Wherever you wind up lying beneath me like this," he said a little savagely as he suddenly rolled on top of her, "is my bed. Can't you understand?" And then he took her parted lips and trapped her legs with his own.

Savannah's determination to take him at his word and ultimately control the heady situation wavered as her body rejoiced in the voluptuousness of the moment. She felt as if he were trying to merge them into one human being, make her a part of him. She sensed the strength and power in him, challenging her not to withhold her own power, and slowly she responded to it, exercising the vitality and smooth coordination of her own strong body.

He was more than a match for her energy and passion, seeming to glory in his ability to release it and then master it. Savannah experienced for the first time in her life the freedom to let the female animal in her battle the male animal in a man. The primeval sexual combat was an incredibly intoxicating thing, unlike anything she had ever known. She couldn't even begin to imagine a man like Jeff Painter or Eric Daly dropping their sophistication long enough to engage in it. For men like them, sex would be something akin to a sport. For Cord Harding it was an affirmation of the life-force. And she responded to it on the most basic feminine level of herself.

"You see?" he grated heavily, taking small, stinging bites as his mouth moved over the slope of her breasts. "You were meant to be mine. We go together, you and I. I need you tonight, my amazon, and I can tell you need me!" His tongue flicked over the tautness of her nipples, making her groan in response and arch her hips against him. "That's what I want from you," he whispered. "Everything you have to give. Don't hold back anything, sweet Savannah. You won't be sorry. . . ." His fingers traced a tantalizing pattern over the skin of her stomach and she sucked in her breath.

"Oh, Cord, I can't let you do this to me," she wailed softly, feeling her feminine strength being seductively mastered. Her head turned aside on the pillow, her fingers laced in the heavy redness of his hair.

"I'm going to make you know me," he vowed. "I want you to know me so completely, you won't be able to look at another man without realizing you belong to me!"

She heard the possessiveness in his voice and sensed the ungovernable masculine instinct behind it. A man like this would own a woman while he wanted her. She would be his. And what would happen to her when he tired of the relationship? a small voice in Savannah's brain demanded frantically. What would happen at the end of the weekend? Desperately she tried to recall the rights he had given her to call a halt to the passionate lovemaking. If she didn't use them and soon, she would be paying her gambling debt in a manner that would scar her for life! She knew now that giving herself to Cord Harding was a risk of previously-unguessed-at proportions. There was too much danger in him, too much undefined menace. She must grab her one chance to escape!

"Cord, no!" she gasped, aware of his lips on the softness of her stomach and of the straying, questing fingers of his hand. "That's enough! You promised!"

For a helpless moment she thought he was going to ignore her. His hands tightened obstinately, as if he would not be halted.

"Savannah, you don't want me to stop and you know it!" he said huskily, lifting his head finally to gaze passionately down into her golden eyes. "Trust me tonight, my sweet. . . ."

"No," she denied on a thread of sound, aware of her vulnerability. "You said I would be the one to call an end to this and I'm—I'm exercising my right . . ." Her voice trailed off in the face of the unremitting hardness in his whole body. He could take her so easily and they both knew it.

"You're going to send me away after all?" he breathed, toying with the rich brown curve of her hair as it fell over her shoulder. "You'd do that to both of us?"

111

"Perhaps you don't know me as well as you thought you did!" she flung back desperately.

"No, I understand full well what's going through that very female mind of yours," he countered, his words deep and almost soothing. "You're going to prove to both of us that you're not weak. That you have no intention of sacrificing your pride to your body's demands. But you don't have to prove anything to me, Savannah. I like this particular weakness in you. I want to be the only one who can generate it!" He leaned forward and kissed her gently, lingeringly. "Don't be afraid of it or me. . . ."

"I'm not afraid!" she retorted, anger fueling her ebbing strength. "I'm simply proving you're not the invincible lover you think you are!"

One red brow lifted at that statement. "Is that right?" he asked evenly. "You think you could resist me now if I chose to disregard your demand?"

"You'll never find out, will you?" she gritted. "Because you're going to leave. You gave me your word!"

"I suppose I did ask for this," he admitted laconically, levering himself up to a sitting position beside her. She saw the heat fading rapidly from the emerald eyes and knew she was winning. "But how long do you think you can keep going?" he went on curiously, touching the tip of her breast with a proprietary finger. "Every night you're going to find yourself in my arms and every night you're going to tell yourself it's all right to give in to the feelings of the moment because in the end you'll be able to send

112

me away. But sooner or later you won't use your prerogative, will you, Savannah? Sooner or later you'll be swept up completely in this thing that exists between us and you'll find yourself waking up in my arms. And then I'll have my promised weekend."

"No!" she challenged valiantly. "I won't give a weekend to a man who sees me only as a conquest!" She edged clear of his hand and slipped off the side of the bed, hurrying to the closet and pulling out a robe. "Now leave," she ordered, frantically tying the sash under his disturbing gaze. "You have to go. You said you would!"

He rose slowly from the rumpled bed, picking up his shirt without a word and buttoning it thoughtfully.

She said nothing, watching fascinated as he adjusted his clothing. He saw her regard and suddenly smiled his feral smile. "It's okay, you know. This is just a temporary delay. I'll still have my weekend and anything else I want from you. You will pay your debt, Savannah, and you'll do it willingly!"

Savannah stared mutely at him as he crossed the room to the door and let himself out into the hall. Without a word he shut the door behind him, leaving her alone to contemplate the chaos of her own emotions.

My God! she thought, sinking woefully down onto the bed, her hands clasped in her lap. *What have I done? What am I doing? I must remember I've won this round,* she told herself fiercely. Cord had been so sure of himself that he had given her the authority to control him and she had used it! Much to his

113

amazement, she felt certain. She let the significance of the action invade her brain. The evening had not concluded as Cord Harding had planned it. Of course it hadn't concluded exactly as she had planned it either, but she couldn't help but feel she had definitely come out ahead. So why did her bed suddenly seem cold and uninviting?

Sexual attraction, Savannah told herself bracingly as she headed for the bathroom to brush her teeth. That's all it was: sexual attraction. Cord was counting on it to bring her to the point where she would be eating out of his hand, but she would show him!

"Brave words, my girl," she said aloud to the image in the mirror. "But what happens the next time things go this far? You very nearly didn't stop him tonight and you know it!"

The thing about being honest with oneself, she decided dismally as she trailed back to the bed, was that it forced one to deal with a problem instead of shelving it. She might as well face the fact that she couldn't take too many nights like this one. Sooner or later she would rationalize the situation to the point where she would, as Cord had promised, find herself waking up in his arms.

Deliberately she forced herself to consider that possibility. What if she gave in and paid her debt? For a moment the tantalizing novelty of the idea enveloped her. If what she experienced in his arms was only a physical thing, perhaps it would be easiest on herself to get it out of her system. Talk about rationalization! It was Cord who would be working her out of his system, not the other way around,

114

instinct warned. She would find herself thoroughly enmeshed in the bonds he could weave so easily around her. *Good Lord,* she thought, blinking in stunned amazement. *I'm in danger of falling in love with the man!*

The simplicity of the realization struck her like a blow. That was the real risk in succumbing to an affair with Cord Harding. She might as well face up to it. He intrigued her, attracted her, made her supremely conscious of him. During the past two months of working for him, she had told herself that her desire to avoid him at the office was because they either wound up arguing or she felt he didn't take her seriously. Her romantic fantasies had been centered on Jeff Painter before Cord had appeared on the scene, and after Jeff had been sent to San Diego, she had refused to contemplate the idea of being disloyal. After all, Jeff had represented everything she thought she wanted in a man. The wave of anger as it became apparent Jeff was finding another interest had dominated her thoughts for several weeks, blinding her to Cord until everything had come to a point last night at the party.

Savannah gave her head a small, dismayed shake as she tugged the sheet up to her chin and lay staring at the ceiling. What a mess! She must be a shallow, superficial little fool to think she was in love with Jeff one minute and the next find herself on the brink of disaster with another man. But it was ludicrous to compare the two sets of emotions. The truth was that what she had felt for Jeff may, indeed, have been shallow and superficial. What she had known tonight with Cord was anything but! And last night had been just as charged with tension and primitive response. What other explanation was there for the way she had sat across a table from Cord Harding and gambled so intently? If the situation had been reversed and it was Cord she were trying to get over, she would never have let Jeff Painter manipulate her into such recklessness. But Cord had done it with ease!

And then the idea came to her. For a moment it seemed so impossible, Savannah wanted to forget it completely. But that proved equally impossible, and for an hour she lay quite still, letting her vivid imagination toy with the notion of what it would be like to make Cord Harding fall in love with her.

What would it be like to have all that masculine desire, that overwhelming male determination aimed at her out of love rather than the wish for a temporary association?

"No," Savannah whispered to herself in the darkness, "it would never work!" But what if it did work? What if she could enlarge his feelings toward her to encompass other emotions besides the physical? Cord was obviously capable of going to a great deal of effort just to secure a woman he wanted only for a weekend. What would it be like if he wanted to marry her?

A feeling of wild recklessness washed over Savannah, not unlike the emotions she had experienced last night when she had gambled for revenge and not unlike the sensations she had known tonight in Cord's arms. It would be a dangerous game to play, she reminded herself grimly. She would have to

116

maintain a strict control over herself while she carefully encouraged Cord. There would be no way to manage it without falling into the vortex herself. She had realized tonight that falling in love with Cord Harding would be an incredibly simple matter. The moment Cord became aware of her weakness, he would move to act on it, taking advantage of her vulnerability to achieve his own goals where she was concerned. She would have to keep him from knowing the truth until she had some inkling of whether or not he was capable of loving her.

Even as she told herself not to be ridiculous the excitement was building along Savannah's nerve endings. There was a curious thrill in the notion of manipulating Cord into something as wild as falling in love with her. She had never known this strange, heedless feeling. In a way it was an extension of last night's recklessness, which she thought on the plane this morning she had dispelled. Determinedly Savannah reminded herself of how disgusted she had been today every time she recalled last night's dangerous games. But now, her body still warm from Cord's caresses, the feelings were back, full-blown. She had never known such rash notions with any other man. Cord had somehow uncovered an unexpected sense of daring she hadn't realized existed in herself.

"Go to sleep, Savannah. Perhaps in the morning sanity will return and you'll realize how crazy all these ideas are!" After a few more sensible words to herself Savannah dutifully shut her eyes and went to sleep.

But the light of the new day didn't bring the

sought-after common sense. Instead she awoke with such a marvelous sensation of impending adventure, it was all Savannah could do to keep from grinning slyly to herself each time she passed a mirror. "You're a fool, my girl!" she made herself say every five minutes. "It will never work. You'll find yourself at his mercy, not the other way around!"

But she would be careful, she promised herself. She would lead Cord on in a subtle, deliberate way, using his obvious physical interest in her as a lure. The image of herself as a siren made Savannah smile. Never had she intentionally set out to play such a role, but suddenly the idea of seeing how far she could go in manipulating Cord was unbelievably exciting! She had never encountered a man who had challenged her in quite the way Cord was challenging her.

There were risks involved, Savannah reminded herself, trying to damp down the sense of expectation with a dose of common sense. But she had his word he wouldn't force the physical side of things, and as long as she kept her head when she was in his arms, she would surely be all right. Something in her shied away from contemplation of what would happen if she lost control of that issue though, something deep and feminine that warned that if she ever allowed Cord to make her his all the fine games would come to an end. If she hadn't succeeded in making him fall in love with her by that time, Savannah knew, she would be lost.

In spite of the new risk-oriented viewpoint, however, the knock on her door as she was buttoning a silky yellow blouse made Savannah jump. She knew at once who would be waiting in the hall and suddenly last night's schemes seemed impossibly farfetched. She was no vamp! How could she pull off a coup of this magnitude? Controlling and manipulating men were the skills of small, fragile blondes, not tall, strong, professional women who had never experienced the heady sensation of men throwing themselves at their feet.

"Courage, Savannah!" she hissed to herself as she tucked the shirt into the waistband of her sleek, fitted jeans. "You haven't spent the past five years in personnel work without learning a thing or two about handling people!" She crossed the room and opened the door cautiously.

"Good morning," Cord greeted her pleasantly enough, his gaze roving over her chicly casual attire with a certain sense of ownership that nettled Savannah. "Ready for breakfast?"

"Where are you staying?" she demanded, saying the first thing she could think of as she took in the picture he made. He was wearing a dark brown shirt with the sleeves rolled nonchalantly up on his forearms and a pair of well-cut slacks that emphasized the lean, powerful build. The thick red hair was still damp from his morning shower and Savannah found herself thinking he looked very good to her. Memories of the previous evening flooded her mind and she had to take a firm grip on her reaction. If Cord was purposefully setting out to make her aware of him, he was becoming very successful!

"Two doors down from you. I toyed with the idea

119

of telling the desk clerk you were my runaway wife and having him book me into your room, but somehow even I was intimidated by the thought of the scene you might make!"

"I assure you I would have raised hell," she informed him loftily. "Furthermore, I wasn't aware I had a date for breakfast with you!"

"Now that you do know, do you think you could get moving?" he returned smoothly. "I'm quite hungry in the mornings, and if my food is delayed too long, I have a tendency to turn downright surly."

Savannah's mouth quirked downward in a wry expression. "As it happens, I'm a little hungry myself. One of the penalties of being built on a grand scale, I suppose—a healthy appetite." She stepped into the hall, shutting the door behind her with a sense of leaving the relative safety of a base camp to go into the front lines of combat.

"Such gracious acceptance of my invitations will go to my head." He grinned.

"Try a truly gracious method of inviting me and you might get a better response! All you did was show up at my door and ask me if I was ready."

"With you I find it's better to take a more forceful approach. By the way, I enjoy having you built on a grand scale. I find I like having a woman who doesn't get lost in the sheets! So it's to my advantage to feed you well, you see."

"Another comment like that," she snapped, flushing furiously, "and you'll be eating alone!"

"Sorry," he said, not sounding at all apologetic. "I'm glad you're an early riser too. I was afraid I'd have to drag you out of bed. Something in common, isn't that nice?" He stopped right in the middle of the stairs and pulled her close. "Good morning, Savannah, my sweet." He bent to kiss her surprised, up-turned face.

"Look out!" she squeaked, afraid of losing her balance on the stair tread.

"Relax." Cord smiled humorously. "I'd never let you fall." He finished his kiss, a thoroughly posses-sive, good-morning kiss that left Savannah breathless in spite of herself. "I would have done that as soon as you opened the door a minute ago, but I'm afraid we would have been very late getting down to break-fast."

"And your food is much more important?" Savan-nah mumbled tartly, trying to ignore the gleam in his green eyes as they resumed their descent.

"Are you implying you'd rather go back to the room?" he inquired interestedly.

"No!"

He chuckled richly as he guided her toward the sunny, glass-walled dining room, which had been designed to give patrons the feeling of breakfasting in a garden. "You know, you missed a great opportu-nity to enjoy one of the world's finest omelets when you got cold feet the other night and left before breakfast."

"I didn't get cold feet!" Savannah retorted, stung. "I never intended to pay that debt and you should have known it! No self-respecting woman would have paid it."

"It's only a matter of time, my sweet," he corrected, seating her. "You'll pay it, one way or another. What will you have for breakfast?" he continued blandly, switching from one topic to the other as if they held the same level of importance in life.

"Freedom from your vindictiveness, I hope," Savannah retorted, reaching for a menu.

"Sweetheart, it's not vindictive to want my winnings," Cord explained patiently as if dealing with a sulky child. "One of these days you'll be honest with both of us and admit it. How about the eggs Benedict?"

Savannah, finding it difficult to keep her mind on food, even though she was quite hungry, nodded shortly. How in the world was she ever going to proceed with her plans? Cord always seemed to be the one in charge when he was anywhere in the vicinity. She needed to gain more control so that she was the one who set the pace of this strange hunt.

"I'd rather you didn't frown at me like that first thing in the morning," Cord remarked blandly. "A quirk in my nature, no doubt, but I prefer your smiles to your frowns."

"You'd better get used to the frowns if you're intent on shadowing me for heaven knows how long," Savannah said sweetly, feeling better.

"There, you see? You can smile at me when you try," he pounced, pleased.

"That sort of expression is usually classified as an acid smile," Savannah noted haughtily, straightening the line of her lips immediately.

"I'll take what I can get for now," he said philosophically. "Perhaps in another few days I'll have managed to elicit something more warming in the way of smiles from you."

"What do you mean, 'another few days'? Just how long are you planning on staying here in Carmel, Cord?" Savannah asked warily.

"After I got back to my room last night, I realized this project might take a bit longer than I had originally planned," he admitted ruefully.

"You didn't think I'd send you away last night, did you?" Savannah observed with satisfaction.

"I've decided to take the same vacation time you're taking," he went on, ignoring her remark. "I'll be spending the next two weeks here in Carmel with you, honey. No matter where you go or what you do, I'll be right there with you, every step of the way."

CHAPTER SIX

Savannah eyed her tormentor in silence for a moment, only the cool tapping of one fingernail on the white tablecloth betraying her inner turmoil. "You can't," she hazarded at last, "simply take two weeks off without making arrangements at the office. You're the boss."

"Which is exactly why I can do it," he laughed. "Rank has its privileges." He was clearly awaiting her reaction to the news that he intended to be underfoot during her entire stay in Carmel.

"A true optimist such as myself learns to look for opportunity in the midst of crisis," she said with a challenging smile. And that was nothing less than the truth, she added silently, encouragingly. What was needed was a plan of attack. She was going to have her opponent in reach for the next couple of weeks. It was time she took herself off the defensive and began organizing an offense.

"An excellent philosophy," Cord approved, eyes glittering with barely suppressed laughter. "I half expected you to announce plans to leave town and try a quick disappearing act."

"Something along the lines of 'this town isn't big enough for both of us'?" she said as the waiter approached to take their order.

"Something along the lines of panic," he corrected when the waiter had been satisfied.

"You underestimate me," she retorted coolly.

"How can you say that? You've already flown the coop once on me!"

"Are you *hoping* I'll run?" she demanded quizzically, tilting her head to one side.

"Oh, no," he denied, grinning broadly. "There's no doubt I'll find matters much less wearing if you stay in one place for a change."

"I'm not staying put to make things easier for you. I'm staying here because I have no intention of letting you ruin my vacation!"

"I trust I shall be able to improve upon it."

"And I trust I shall be able to demonstrate that I'm not under your domineering thumb!" she stated firmly, feeling the excitement beginning to build inside as she deliberated her potential courses of action.

"Under my thumb is not exactly where I want you," he chuckled. "I prefer the position you were in last night." He broke off, watching with evident pleasure as Savannah turned a bright pink. "What would you like to do after breakfast?" he went on imperturbably, as if he'd just made some comment on the weather.

A plan of attack, Savannah thought grimly. She needed a mapped-out scheme with a logical approach to the problem. Something to make him aware of her as she was rapidly becoming aware of him. A plan that would make him want her for more than just a weekend affair. Cord Harding was going to learn to see her as more than a passing challenge! Or else she must convince herself that there was no hope of deepening his feelings beyond his present state of desire.

What were the traditional, tried and true methods women had utilized so effectively down through the years when they attempted to engage a man's interest and explore the extent of his passion? Then it came to her. The simplest, most basic tactic that could tell her a great deal about the potential status of Cord's feelings. Jealousy. She would try to make him jealous and observe his reactions. He had mentioned his own possessiveness but how deep did it go and at what point would it become outright jealousy?

"I'm not sure what I'll be doing after breakfast," Savannah informed him blandly but with the distinct feeling of finally having made her first countermove in this strange and risky game. "I'm expecting a call from Eric."

"Fine," he responded equally blandly. "I'm sure the three of us can find something to talk about during a morning walk."

Not the most promising of reactions, Savannah

decided, wishing she could read his thoughts more clearly in those gray-green eyes. "I'm not inviting you to join us," she murmured pointedly as the eggs Benedict were set before her.

"Come now," he admonished, examining his own plate with relish. "You're not going to be rude to a visiting friend, are you?"

"If you're the visiting friend, I'm afraid so. I know you'll understand," Savannah told him dryly. "After all, with Jeff out of my life I mustn't waste time looking for a replacement. Not at my age."

"Good grief! You're surely not making altar plans for poor Eric already, are you? After only one date?" He looked properly scandalized, and Savannah would have laughed if she hadn't been so busy formulating her next moves.

"A woman has to keep her options open. Eric *may* turn out to be just a vacation fling, but the possibility of more is there," she explained politely.

"I see," Cord said dryly, munching thoughtfully while he studied her composed features. "Why don't you tell yourself that about me and then we can begin exploring the—uh—possibilities?"

"No, you've already made it clear you're only looking for a weekend affair," Savannah noted, shaking her head. "Besides, there's something quite attractive about Eric. He's a very successful real estate type, you know."

"No, I didn't know. I was sitting a little too far away from the table last night to participate in the conversation," Cord remarked with the smallest hint of grimness.

"Well, he is. He's from the San Francisco Bay area and you know how much more sophisticated Northern Californians are compared to us Southern Californians! Such a relief to find a man who doesn't wear pale blue loafers and a matching belt!" She smiled brilliantly across the table.

"Don't say that as if you've ever seen me wearing such things," Cord warned with an amused chuckle. "I don't even own a pair of pale blue loafers, much less the matching belt!"

"Nevertheless I'm sure you get the picture."

"You know what I think?" Cord announced smoothly. "I think you're finding this Eric attractive because he reminds you of Jeff Painter. A bad mistake, you realize, trying to replace one wrong man with another just like him."

Savannah blinked, a bit surprised that he'd seen the same superficial similarities between Jeff and Eric, but she managed a shrug and an unconcerned smile.

"I'm old enough to choose my own men, thank you. If I feel the need of advice, I'll be certain to call on you, however." Savannah set down her fork and placed her napkin on the table. "Now, if you don't mind, I believe I'll be going back up to my room. I hope you enjoy your day as much as I intend to enjoy mine."

"No reason why I shouldn't since I intend to be right behind you."

"Perhaps I'll suggest to Eric that we take a drive," Savannah threatened lightly. "You'd find it a bit difficult to follow us in that event!"

"Oh, I don't know. Where are the logical places to drive around here? Seventeen-Mile Drive through Del Monte Forest? The Big Sur area? Over to Monterey? All slow, meandering, sight-seeing trips where it would be easy to keep you in sight. I've still got my rental car so there shouldn't be any trouble. Of course, it might be difficult explaining to Eric why he's being followed. I have a better idea for you if you're determined to spend the day with him. Stay in Carmel and I'll remain unobtrusively in the background. Much easier on both of us. How's that?" Cord concluded cheerfully.

Savannah frowned severely at him, wondering what made him think he could ever fade quietly into any background. With his build and that brilliant red hair, Cord would stand out in any environment, and he must have known it.

"You'll give me your word not to pester us?" she probed, turning ideas over in her mind.

"Not until the magic hour of ten o'clock when your coach turns back into a pumpkin," he promised with a dazzling smile.

"You're expecting me to call another evening short? If I wind up spending the evening with Eric, that is?" she demanded coldly, lifting one dark brow quellingly.

"Naturally. The basic tactic of my approach to conditioning you is to make certain you say all your good-nights in my arms, remember?" Cord reached for the last piece of toast as if totally unconcerned about her reaction.

Savannah, on inspiration, stifled the tirade that

hovered on the tip of her tongue, said nothing at all, but flashed her best laughing smile and rose from her seat, turning to leave.

"Savannah," he called from behind her in silken tones eminently full of danger.

"Yes?" She paused, mockingly polite.

"You do realize I'm quite serious about all this, don't you? I wouldn't want you to get the wrong impression just because I've done something soft and time-wasting like allowing you a certain amount of latitude."

"Where would I get the wrong impression? You've made yourself very clear," she said coolly, waiting.

"I just wanted to be certain. For a moment or two there I thought I saw the same look in those interesting eyes of yours that I saw the other night while you were gambling. As if you thought we were still playing games."

"Aren't we?" she asked saucily.

"Only in one respect, honey," he drawled. "I'm going to win again."

Savannah swept out of the dining room without a backward glance, her head set regally, her long graceful stride moving her quickly out of Cord's sight.

The rest of the day developed into a cat-and-mouse situation, which nearly made Savannah want to scream at times. Eric did, indeed, call as promised, and together they spent the afternoon touring the countless boutiques and craft shops that lined Carmel's main street.

In such a small village it was ridiculously easy for

Cord to appear at odd moments during the day. Savannah would step out of a shop, Eric behind her, and nearly collide with Cord's massive form as he was in the process of entering. She would be studying a piece of pottery and, out of the corner of her eye, see Cord buying a small item at the counter. Occasionally he waved cheerfully from across the street, like an old friend.

"Isn't that the fellow who was in the hall last night when I brought you back to the inn?" Eric asked at one point, a small frown of remembrance creasing his brow as Cord disappeared ahead of them into an artist's shop.

"Yes, I guess he's looking for that mantel art he mentioned," Savannah responded glibly, wondering what Cord was thinking as he went through the motions of their latest game. He didn't seem particularly upset by the sight of her with Eric. Rather there had been a sort of patient, waiting quality about him that spoke volumes for his self-confidence but didn't indicate anything as primitive and basic as jealousy!

Very deliberately Savannah allowed her hand to brush Eric's. He reacted right on cue, catching her fingers between his and smiling at her engagingly. It was just too bad, she thought, returning the smile, that she was beginning to find her new acquaintance somewhat boring. But she made certain she was standing comfortably in the circle of Eric's arm, studying the contents of a bookstore window when Cord next appeared on the street beside them. For all the good it did, she groaned to herself as he merely greeted them both and went on past. The only expression she caught in the gray-green eyes as they momentarily meshed with hers was outright laughter.

During the afternoon she went to the windswept beach with Eric, where she was treated to a long discussion of some of his more brilliant real estate ventures. He was a pleasant enough man, Savannah told herself, but she simply couldn't get excited at the prospect of having dinner with him, an invitation she knew would probably be forthcoming soon. On the other hand, she needed his assistance. . . .

It was at that point that Savannah finally acknowledged to herself the necessity of manipulating not one but two men in order to achieve her desired goal. A very disquieting thought and one that made her feel the beginning of guilt pangs.

In spite of her qualms, however, ten o'clock found Savannah dancing in Eric's arms in the lounge of her inn. It was he who had suggested the location, not she, and Savannah was tense, half expecting Cord to announce the arrival of the witching hour in some humiliating fashion. Each minute past ten seemed an eternity to her, even while she smiled and tried to chat pleasantly with Eric. There was no sign of Cord.

"Would you like to go outside for the traditional breath of fresh air?" Eric grinned meaningfully around ten fifteen. "It's getting a bit close in here and there's nothing as effective as a sea breeze and moonlight—"

"As effective for what?" Savannah said lightly, not really wanting to go outside with him, but knowing it was the next intelligent move in her scheme.

133

"Let's find out, shall we?" he suggested, leading her toward the French doors that opened out onto a charming garden terrace.

Savannah glanced at him and nearly frowned. Eric was wearing that familiar male look of anticipation, and she knew exactly what to expect out on the terrace. Well, she was a big girl in more ways than one and at the moment she needed Eric's attention. She only wished Cord would appear in time to catch the moonlight kiss that was coming. . . .

"I've had a very enjoyable day, Savannah," Eric was saying, massaging the back of her neck with what she supposed was a sensuous motion. Its main effect was to make her want to step out of reach. With a sigh she restrained herself and answered him pleasantly. Where was Cord? It would be ten thirty soon.

"So have I, Eric. You've given me a great start on my vacation." Savannah yawned very delicately. "I think you're right about this sea breeze, by the way. It is having a certain influence! Either that or the long walk we took this afternoon is!"

"Sleepy again?" he chuckled, his mouth hovering close. "Perhaps it's time you went to bed," he added deliberately, and then he kissed her.

Savannah accepted the kiss and the masculine pass with good grace, she thought, marveling at the lack of excitement in Eric's caress. If Cord had achieved nothing else, he had certainly spoiled her for the average moonlight kiss, she thought grimly.

"You're a very interesting woman, Savannah," Eric said, moving to deepen the kiss that she was

134

beginning to find tedious. "I'm glad we ran into each other on the beach yesterday." His lips nuzzled the corner of her mouth and Savannah wanted very badly to put an end to the embrace.

What if her short time with Cord had ruined more than just the average kiss? she reflected with an unpleasant feeling. What if it went deeper than that and her redheaded pursuer had inflicted himself so indelibly on her consciousness that she would spend the rest of her life comparing other men to him?

No! She promised herself almost violently she was going to win the game. Cord Harding was going to learn the difference between love and lust.

"I'd invite you back to the house," Eric murmured suggestively in her ear, "but I'm afraid my friends are at home tonight. . . ." He let the sentence trail off on an inquiring note.

"And you're hoping I'll offer my room instead?" Savannah said dryly, wondering if modern man felt he could be less gallant with modern woman simply because she wasn't as protected by her family as she had been in past ages.

"The thought did occur to me." Eric smiled expectantly, apparently misreading the mild amusement in her slightly narrowed eyes for passion.

Savannah opened her mouth to tell him quite clearly that, while she had enjoyed the evening, she had no intention of involving herself in a torrid vacation affair. And just as quickly shut it again as movement inside the lounge caught her attention. Even in the shadowy light she could see the red hair and massive build. Cord! This was her chance. . . .

135

"I'm—I'm not sure, Eric," she said, trying to put the proper degree of hesitation into her words. "After all, we've just met and—" She looked at him appealingly, trying to project the need to be convinced. She wanted his next kiss to come at the appropriate moment.

"I think we're going to have a very good time together." Eric smiled encouragingly, leaning close to respond to the offer of her slightly parted lips.

Savannah told herself she'd worry later about any false impressions she might have been creating. Only one thing counted at that moment and that was the timing of this embrace!

Eric's hands went around her and she knew there was a certain amount of undeniable expertise in his kiss, but it stirred no answering response in her. All she could think about was whether or not Cord had a view of the terrace scene.

Over the top of Eric's shoulder she saw her opponent as he stepped through the glass doors onto the terrace, headed straight toward the couple. The very blandness of his expression was dismaying. In fact it looked suspiciously like humor flickering in the sea-colored eyes, Savannah decided unhappily. Definitely not jealousy!

"There you are, Miss Emery," Cord declared cheerfully, coming to a halt beside Eric as the younger man, slightly flustered, released Savannah. "The desk clerk has been looking all over for you. Told him if I saw you I'd give you the message."

"What message?" Savannah asked with deep suspicion. Cord's mien was entirely too innocent.

"Why, that your husband called and said he'll be arriving on the six-thirty plane tomorrow morning," Cord finished with a helpful tone in his voice. Only Savannah saw the hint of a mildly savage grin under the well-mannered smile.

"Her husband!" Eric exclaimed, clearly shocked.

"What?" Savannah demanded, just as amazed. She flashed Cord a seething, vengeful glance and then turned to Eric who was rapidly putting distance between himself and his date for the evening.

"Eric, listen to me," she snapped, impatient with his cowardice.

"You said you weren't married!" he accused, ignoring the bringer of the bad news in favor of the one who had plainly lied. "Arriving on the six-thirty flight, for God's sake! He probably would have walked in and found us in bed!" Eric seemed dazed by the near miss. "I suppose you were just looking for a little fun until your husband arrived, but it was hardly fair to use me like that!"

"Oh, do shut up, will you?" she hissed waspishly, aware of Cord's avid interest in the proceedings and wishing she could spend the time yelling at him instead of Eric. "You were quite happy to use *me*, don't forget! You wanted me to invite you up to my room."

"That was before—" Eric began protestingly, backing away from the increasing wrath in Savannah's furiously frowning face.

"Don't try and pretend your intentions were in any way honorable!" she snarled. "In fact I seriously doubt if either of you knows the meaning of the word!" She swiveled, including Cord in her tirade. Eric edged further away as he realized someone else was about to bear the brunt of the lecture. "You're both alike, aren't you? Both out for whatever you can get as long as you don't have to pay too high a price! A weekend affair, a vacation affair—who cares? A little fun and that's the end of it. Well, you can both go to hell, do you hear me? And you might as well go there together because you'll have so much to talk about on the way! I'm sure you'll have a great time discussing past flings with women you've known! But you know something? I'll bet most of those women have forgotten both of you! After all, when men are so similar, it's hard to keep them sorted out in one's mind! That's right, Eric, run off into the night like a coward! See if I care!" Savannah concluded, stamping a foot fiercely in angry frustration as one of her victims fled the terrace.

"I'm still here," Cord put in helpfully, as Savannah glared after her erstwhile escort for the evening. "You can yell at me as much as you like, I won't run away, honey."

"As for you, Cord Harding, you should be ashamed of yourself for telling such lies!" Savannah whirled around to face him again, her hands planted on her hips, her brows drawn together in a ferocious expression. "Look what you've done! You've ruined my whole evening!"

"I did warn you that after ten things were going to turn pumpkiny." He grinned unabashedly, clearly pleased with the effects of his small announcement of a few moments ago. "And how can you say I've ruined your evening anyway when I saved you from having to fend off your friend's advances?"

"You can wipe that stupid grin off your face," she informed him nastily. "Who said I wanted him fended off?"

"Now you're the one telling lies." He chuckled good-naturedly, reaching out his hand to stroke the side of her cheek almost fondly and appearing not to notice when she made a small production out of turning her head aside. "I saw the look in your eyes. You weren't concentrating on Daly's kiss at all."

"How do you know?" she challenged.

"In the first place your eyes would have been closed if you'd been about to swoon with passion, not wide open and watching me!" he chided. "Second . . . well, never mind. Suffice it to say I know I did you a favor. And it *was* after ten, sweetheart," he reminded her as if she'd accidentally forgotten the fact. "And I made it clear we're playing this game by my rules. Did you think I'd let you get away with breaking them?"

"The rules of the game!" she echoed scathingly. "That's how you see this entire mess, isn't it? A game! Men! I'd just as soon not see either you or Eric again as long as I live!"

"Finished?" Cord inquired politely. "Because if you are, I'd like to take the opportunity to point out that I'm a hell of a lot different from your friend Daly and I'm beginning to resent being compared to him."

"Name one way in which you're different!" she said, outraged.

"The fact that I'm still standing here waiting for

you to simmer down while he's long gone should be enough to convince you there's a fundamental difference in our makeup!" Cord grinned wickedly.

"So?" Savannah grated. "The only difference I can see is that you're a little more persistent!"

"I'm a *lot* more persistent, my dear. I am, as it happens, fully determined to win this 'game.'" He took her arm, his fingers tightening in warning as she tried to pull away. "I differ in a few other ways too," he went on with a knowing look. "Ways you should be aware of now that I've let you kiss him."

"You didn't *let* me kiss him!" she stormed rashly. "I encouraged him to kiss me! I wanted him to kiss me!" He was leading her toward the shadowy entrance to the lounge and the small voice of common sense noted that she would have to do something or be led straight up to bed. But her temper was still in full sail and it was difficult to think of anything but arguing with the insufferable creature. It was frustrating enough to have her plans collapse, but to have Cord claiming she'd only kissed Eric because she'd been *allowed* to do so was downright infuriating.

"I saw you heading out here with him a few minutes ago. Thought I'd give you a little time to make comparisons, as it were, and convince yourself that you're only really at home in *my* arms—"

"Well," she interrupted with forced coolness, "as long as I'm going to be allowed to make comparisons before ten o'clock in the evening, I expect I can live with you haunting me until such time as you grow tired of the game. A lot can happen before ten o'clock if a woman plans well!" Was there no hope at all? she wondered dismally. Hadn't Cord been in the least bit jealous?

"Forget it," he advised with an amused sideways glance. "I'm discovering I don't like playing the patient lover. If you want to maintain the rights I gave you to choose the time and place of our weekend, you'd better stop encouraging the stray Eric Dalys of this world."

Savannah sneaked a thoughtful glimpse of his profile, wondering if she had managed to strike a small vein of genuine jealousy somewhere in that large frame. "So long as I'm back by ten, I'm playing by your rules, aren't I?" she asked saucily as he steered her through the lounge and out into the lobby.

"I just changed the rules slightly," he murmured smoothly.

"Hardly fair," she sniffed, realizing she was going to have to do something and quickly. Cord showed every sign of heading straight back to her room. There was a familiar aspect of single-mindedness about him at the moment that she knew she'd better find a way to handle.

"Nobody promised a lot of fairness, just a lot of rules," he retorted. He had one foot on the bottom step of the stairs leading to the room floor when he finally became aware of the fact that Savannah was hanging back.

"Now what?" he asked with impatience, looking down into her rebellious features.

"I'm not ready to go back to the room yet."

"No? What would you like to do?" he queried mockingly. It was infuriating that he could laugh at her, she thought, even while he was getting ready to stage another seduction scene.

"I would like another drink in the lounge," she responded, making the first suggestion that came to mind. "Perhaps a few more dances," she added belligerently. "This is supposed to be my vacation, remember?"

"I remember," he agreed with an unexpected softness, removing his foot from the step and starting back toward the lounge. "It's mine too. I'm willing to spend a little time on the romantic side of this affair—"

"We're not having an affair!" She felt compelled to remind him even though she was busy with plans now that she'd bought some extra time.

"If you're going to spend the rest of the evening arguing . . ." he threatened kindly.

"I won't," she assured him hurriedly as they found a table. "Even though I've certainly got grounds," she added just under her breath.

Cord magnanimously ignored the muttered comment and ordered the drinks. "I believe you said you wanted to dance?" he remarked, getting to his feet as soon as the liqueurs had been served.

Savannah hesitated, sensing a certain danger in his arms tonight. But there wasn't any option if she wanted to stall a while before dealing with the inevitable bedroom scene. Without a word she rose and allowed him to lead her onto the small dance floor where a few other couples drifted in time to the slow romantic music.

Cord's arms closed around her with the masterful

grip she remembered so well from the last time he had danced with her, and her traitorous body began to relax against him almost immediately as if it recognized home port. Sensing the small surrender, Cord tightened his hold, drawing her closer to him and gently pushing her head down onto his shoulder. Savannah was aware of the satisfaction in him even as her cheek brushed the fine material of his jacket, but she really didn't feel like fighting it. What harm would there be in a few dances? And it was so pleasant being in the arms of a man designed for her size!

"You see how nice things can be when you stop fighting me?" Cord whispered enticingly into her ear, his breath warm on her skin. "Why do you want to go and waste time with men like Eric Daly? We're going to be happy together, you and I."

Savannah stirred and sighed softly. "Eric said something like that too," she observed thoughtfully and felt him stiffen. Had she angered him? she wondered hopefully. "Men are so good at making promises, but at my age a woman should learn to distinguish the truth, don't you think?"

"If she can," he grated a little harshly. "Some women need guidance in such matters!"

"From an older and wiser male?" she suggested demurely.

"In this case, yes! Savannah, for your own sake, don't mention Eric Daly again. You've already tried my patience sorely enough for one evening!"

Savannah felt the strength of his fingers as they moved questingly against the curve of her lower back. What was going through his mind? Irritation or a flicker of real jealousy? He was so strong, she reflected half dreamily, but so far he'd never used that strength to hurt her. What might he do if he was incited to such a fierce passion as the one she was attempting to bring forth? Playing with fire again, that's what she was doing, Savannah lectured herself. But how else was she ever going to find out if there was something more to Cord's interest in her than the challenge of making her pay off her damn gambling debt?

"That's better," he murmured as she failed to make a snappish retort to his warning. "I like your quick tongue, honey, but there's a time and a place for everything!"

Savannah even managed to resist retaliating to that remark and was rewarded by the increased intimacy of his hold. This sort of thing was addicting, she decided grimly. A woman could find herself making all sorts of silly excuses for paying her debts!

It was the sound of a noisy group of people preparing to leave the lounge some time later that finally jarred Savannah into formulating some plans. Cord had just reseated her at the table and was smiling down at her with that anticipatory expression that told her so clearly what he was thinking. She gave herself a small shake, pulled herself together, and acted.

"If you don't mind," she suggested softly, not quite meeting his eyes, "I think I'd like to go up to the room now."

"As I've been looking forward all day to the pleasure of taking you upstairs tonight, I can hardly complain," he told her in a seductive, husky voice that seemed to set up a vibration of sorts deep inside Savannah.

Dammit!, she told herself angrily, *I'm the hunter, not the hunted! I've got to stop reacting like the prey every time he gets that glitter in his eyes!*

The noisy group she wanted to follow was spilling out of the lounge into the lobby. Several members of it, she knew, had rooms on her floor. With any luck they would be heading for the same staircase toward which Cord was aiming.

"Are you nervous, Savannah?" Cord suddenly asked on a whimsical note. The grip on her arm had a gentle relentlessness about it that should have made her *very* nervous.

"Of course not, why should I be nervous? I'm in charge of our goodnights, aren't I?" she retorted with smiling flippancy.

"Perhaps I'm asking the question because I'm a little nervous," he shot back ruefully.

"You!" she exclaimed, glancing up at him in vast surprise. "I don't believe it. I've never seen you nervous!" She thought of his calm, cool approach to the most major of crises at work and shook her head to emphasize her feelings.

"I expect I'm feeling a trifle wary of your inner resolution," he explained politely.

"You mean after what happened last night?" she guessed, experiencing a shaft of pleased satisfaction.

"I've never been one for taking cold showers. Especially when I know they're entirely unnecessary." He chuckled.

The couples Savannah had recognized were ascending the stairs ahead of herself and Cord. The timing would be close and everything depended on it.

"Perhaps," she observed dryly, "I might be less full of resolution if I thought there was a chance you *were* nervous."

"Because knowing I'm feeling uncertain will make you feel more in control?" he hazarded perceptively.

"You're so depressingly self-confident about everything you do! And so persistent! Not just in this crazy game you're forcing me to play, but in business, the way you deal with people, everything!" she complained.

"Funny"—he grinned cheerfully—"I had the same impression about you! A woman who should be approached aggressively if a man wanted to be certain you would ultimately respect him. . . ."

But Savannah wasn't listening any longer. Her whole attention was focused on the laughing, slightly drunken group ahead of them. Deftly she palmed her keys from the small bag she carried and watched for an opening. At the top of the stairs everyone came to a milling halt while two of the couples deliberated the matter of whose room to use for the evening nightcap.

As Cord began politely edging a path around the boisterous group, Savannah managed to disengage herself and circle the gaggle of guests on the other side. For a precious moment or two she was alone.

Standing in front of her door, she slipped the key into the lock, glancing briefly back over her shoulder in time to see Cord freeing himself from the human logjam and starting toward her. She met his eyes and for a split second there was an open line of communication between them. Cord was abruptly aware of her intention, and Savannah knew she was going to get away with it. Suddenly she felt extraordinarily lighthearted and supremely in command.

She smiled at him, her warm, laughing, challenging smile, and stepped into the room, locking the door swiftly behind her.

CHAPTER SEVEN

Step two of the plan to make Cord jealous occurred to Savannah almost as soon as she awoke the next morning. She wasted no time after her shower in dialing the front desk and placing her request.

"That's right. One red rose. Long stemmed. Have the florist deliver it around six o'clock this evening, please. Oh, and I mustn't forget the card...." Savannah thought furiously. She wanted something with just the right touch of passion. "Have the card read 'I made a terrible mistake. Is there any chance for us?' and sign it Jeff. Got that? I certainly appreciate it. I know the request is somewhat unusual. Yes, thank you very much." Savannah hung up the phone, a pleased smile on her face, just as a knock came on her door.

Hastily she jumped to her feet, checking her cool appearance in the mirror as she headed toward the

149

door. The day promised to be warm once the morning fog had burned off, and she had chosen a summery cotton sheath patterned in bold yellow and orange flowers worn with a pair of sandals. On a whim she had elected to leave her sleek brown hair free to fall in a deep curve around her shoulders. The dark mass was anchored back over each ear with two colorful combs.

She opened the door precisely as Cord was about to knock again and smiled up brilliantly at him as he managed to restrain himself and lower his hand.

"Good morning, Cord. Did we have another date for breakfast that I've forgotten?"

"How did you guess?" he inquired smoothly, stepping into the room before she could step out into the hall. His fingers closed around the edge of the door and he pushed it shut behind him. "But there are one or two things we should discuss before we go downstairs," he added drawlingly, the hooded green gaze sweeping over her cheerfully clad figure, giving no hint of whether or not he was holding a grudge from last night.

"Such as?" she asked lightly, trying to mask the vague unease his large presence in the small room gave her. For something casual to do, she waved him politely to the one chair and seated herself on the edge of the bed, watching him with wide, innocent eyes.

"Such as how close you came to exploring the ends of my patience last night," he murmured, leaning back in the chair and studying her features intently. "It was bad enough to find you giving away kisses I

150

have to work at getting out of you, but to have you turn into a complete coward at your door was too much."

"Is that so?" Savannah said interestedly, tipping her head to one side as she eyed him. "I wasn't aware my action upset you. After all, you didn't pound on my door or institute a large-scale fuss."

"Was that what you wanted me to do?" he asked curiously.

"No! Of course not!" she assured him feelingly, mentally conjuring up an image of the scene that would have caused in front of the crowd in the hall.

"I didn't think so. I let you have your little victory last night out of deference to your pride. You looked so damn pleased with your maneuver, I didn't have the heart to embarrass you by demanding admittance."

Savannah blinked in concealed surprise. She had been certain the reason Cord hadn't made a scene at the door was because of his own male pride. It hadn't occurred to her he might have been refraining from the pursuit because of her feelings on the matter! "You're too kind," she mocked lightly, but somehow she found herself believing him.

"Yes, I'm beginning to think I am," he remarked lazily. "I gave you some time and some freedom out of the kindness of my heart and you're abusing both severely." The narrowed, thoughtful gray-green eyes flickered with warning. "I think I'd better shorten the reins a little or risk having you become totally unmanageable!" He didn't move but Savannah wanted to run. It took all her willpower to remain seated, a polite, mocking expression on her face.

"What?" she made herself say lightly. "You're going to change the rules again? I don't know how you expect me to possibly keep one jump ahead of you in this game if you're going to resort to that sort of underhanded tactic!"

"I'm not interested in playing a fair game, only a winning game. I thought I'd mentioned that already. The only reason I'm having to rewrite rules for you is because you have insisted on bending the current ones. Yesterday," he informed her with a hint of reproach, "was a very difficult day for me!"

"Poor Cord," Savannah said sympathetically.

"I agree. Therefore I'm sure you'll understand when I tell you I don't intend to spend another one like it," he drawled.

Savannah waited suspiciously, wondering what was coming.

"I've decided I can do my haunting better if we spend our vacation days together. The business of following you from a distance and being forced to watch you flirt with another man isn't working out very well, you see."

Hope flared to life in Savannah. This certainly was some indication of jealousy, wasn't it? "I hardly think you've given it a fair shot yet," she argued carefully.

He got to his feet in a surge of unexpected power that alarmed Savannah. She rose quickly, trying to put some distance between herself and Cord. He didn't appear angry, only coolly determined. "Now,

Cord," she began placatingly as he moved toward her.

"Now, Savannah," he mimicked, reaching out to snag her bare arm and haul her gently toward him. "Let me outline the new, revised instructions for you."

"I don't think I want to hear them," she protested bravely, aware of the strong fingers on her shoulders, holding her quite firmly. She watched him bravely through her lashes, knowing she was going to have to be careful.

"We will spend our days here in Carmel together," he began briskly, ignoring her attempt at protest. "You will not pick up any more stray men such as Eric Daly and you will give me your undivided attention so that I can get on with the process of making you pay your debts. There, isn't that simple and clear cut?" he added, the hint of a smile in his eyes as he held her a few inches away and watched her expression.

"Very," she conceded dryly, aware that this was exactly the sort of opportunity she needed. Cord's plans could be made to work both ways, to serve his purposes and her own. She needed the time to find some common ground between them, something on which to build the basis of more than an affair.

"Remind me to add 'understands and follows instructions well' to your personnel file when we get back to work," Cord whispered, pulling her against him and lowering his head to take her lips in that commandeering way Savannah was coming to know so well. For a long, sensuous moment she felt her mouth crushed effortlessly beneath his, knew that if he continued she would once again find herself reacting to the sexual dominance and mastery he used so effectively. Then he lifted his head, plainly satisfied.

"What makes you think," she breathed tauntingly, seeking some retaliation for his almost casual aggression, "that you'll be able to put the part about 'follows instructions well' into my file?" Her head tipped back, she leaned against the circle of his arm and forced a deliberate, provocative smile. The tawny eyes reflected her determination not to be completely subservient.

"You'll learn to do as I say," he returned dangerously, his fingers sinking warningly into the softness of her waist. "After all, you'll have me there to provide full-time guidance and direction. How can you go wrong?"

"But if I do . . . ?" she said rashly.

"Be careful, Savannah," he drawled with a slow, slashing grin. "I wasn't given red hair for no purpose!"

"Are you threatening me, Cord?" she demanded in mocking disbelief.

"How perceptive of you, my sweet. Of course I'm threatening you. It's called winning by intimidation, didn't you know? Or is that school of management theory still being taught to aspiring personnel directors?"

"Only as an example of an outmoded style that should be guarded against at all costs!"

"Because it's so effective. Come along now like a good girl and let's get some breakfast. I know you

154

must be hungry, too, and you can continue your little skirmishes just as easily over ham and eggs." He took her by the arm, hauling her easily to the door and out into the hall. "After we eat, you can help me look for the certain something I need over the mantel," he went on conversationally as he used her key to lock the door.

"You were serious about that?" she asked in surprise, remembering how he had conducted a small discussion of his search for such an item the night before last when Eric had brought her back to the room.

"Definitely," he nodded, smiling cheerfully as they descended the stairs. "You've seen the house. Briefly, I admit, but you did see it. Kind of a Spanish motif, according to the interior decorator."

"The decorator? When did you move into the place?" Savannah asked, remembering the elegant leather furniture and the beamed ceilings.

"A couple of months ago. But I let the decorator go before she'd quite finished the job. Everything was getting too formal-looking and I wanted a home, not a showplace. The last thing she told me before she went out the door was to at least put something over the mantel. Too much plain white wall showing, she claimed." Cord shrugged. "Carmel should be as good a place as any to pick up whatever one hangs over a mantel. And your taste seems excellent," he added, startling Savannah.

"What makes you say that?" she asked as they entered the dining room.

"Your taste in everything except men, I suppose

155

I should say," he chuckled, seating her. "But once I've trained that aspect to perfection I shall be able to rely on you for everything."

"Cord, I asked you a question," Savannah persisted firmly.

"About how I know your taste to be good? Since taste is such a personal thing, I suppose I ought to have said that it's compatible with mine, rather than that it's excellent," he said consideringly, as if dealing with a point of philosophy.

"Cord!"

"One of the things I admire about you, my sweet Savannah," he said smoothly, "is that once you've started along a certain path, you keep going to the end or until something major deflects you! All right, I'll satisfy your curiosity. What do I know about your taste? I know you dress well, I know you like classical music, namely Mozart and Vivaldi, and I'm aware of the fact that you have a taste for zinfandel and Chardonnay wines. From California, naturally, and preferably Northern California. I'm also aware that you read science fiction and the good, solid, adventuresome kind at that. . . ."

"How do you know all this?" Savannah asked, staring, her menu forgotten.

"Partly from observation," he began slowly, gray-green eyes gleaming.

"And the rest?" she prodded, frowning suspiciously.

"A few discreet questions dropped here and there among people who know you," he retorted easily.

"Cord Harding! Do you mean to tell me you actually inquired about my—my likes and dislikes? You talked to my friends about me?" Savannah didn't know whether to be totally outraged or completely astounded.

"I was extremely subtle about it, I assure you," he said soothingly. "Give me some credit."

"Credit!" she hissed. "What I ought to give you is this glass of ice water! Right over the top of your head!"

"Restrain yourself, sweetheart," he advised humorously. "Think of the scene."

"I *think,*" she stated clearly, "the scene would be bearable, at least on my part!"

"What?" he asked in laughing surprise. "You think you'd be unaffected by the embarrassment of finding yourself being turned over my knee right out here in front of God and the waiter?"

"You wouldn't dare!"

"No more so than you would dare throw the water all over me," he agreed cheerfully.

"A standoff," Savannah groaned ruefully. "But why did you bother to ask about my preferences?" She deliberately damped down the rising flicker of hope his admission had awakened.

"I never like to go into any new endeavor unprepared," he said wryly.

"You *planned* this weekend you're trying to maneuver me into? Before Jeff's engagement party? Do you always invest so much effort in pursuing short-term affairs?" Savannah asked, the inner hope flaring even higher.

"No." Then Cord smiled straight at her and

Savannah knew she would sink to any depth in her scheming to win this game.

"You think a weekend with me is going to be something special?" she inquired with a certain degree of tartness, meant to convey total lack of interest.

"An experience to remember," he confirmed.

Savannah, who had wanted him to show some interest in a more indefinite arrangement, not just the infamous weekend, hid a small wince.

"You honestly think you can persuade me to go along with this?"

"Oh, yes," he stated categorically, shifting his glance to the approaching waiter.

"Without the use of force?" she persisted, lowering her voice so the waiter wouldn't overhear. She wanted to keep that particular game rule straight.

"Unless I'm unduly provoked," Cord qualified dryly. Then the waiter was upon them.

In spite of the strange thread of tension Savannah experienced in Cord's presence, the morning passed in a remarkably pleasant fashion, she reflected later. The tension was a peculiar thing, making her feel like the hunter one moment, the hunted the next, as if she were involved in a precarious, ever-shifting chess game.

"Well, what do you think?" Cord asked shortly before lunch as they stood together in a small shop and studied an elaborate modern metal sculpture designed to represent a flaring sun.

"I don't think it's what you want. It looks all right in this shop but it's not going to do much for your mantel," Savannah opined thoughtfully. "There's no need to rush the decision," she added without pausing to realize exactly what she was saying. "We're going to be here a couple of weeks and we can take some time to drive over to Monterey before we make a final choice. There are a lot of interesting shops along the old Cannery Row. . . ."

"You're quite right, we have the time." Cord smiled meaningfully, taking her hand in a grip that didn't invite resistance. Savannah, sensing the strength of it, wisely didn't try.

They lunched in a charming Scandinavian sandwich shop, where the fresh flowers on the table reminded Savannah of her own floral arrangement for the coming evening. Would the romantic red rose and the fake note from Jeff succeed in wiping that look of masculine complacency from Cord's eyes? After the episode with Eric she thought she knew enough to guess Cord would react without any great degree of violence, and that was just as well, she admitted privately. For, while it might be reassuring on one hand to know that he was beginning to care enough to respond vigorously to her latest provocation, the fact remained he was awfully large. . . . She would be satisfied with simply heightening his awareness yet another notch. An awareness that, with any luck, went deeper than challenge or desire.

"What are you thinking about?" Cord asked suddenly, interrupting the speculative flow of Savannah's thoughts just as she was about to sink her neat teeth delicately into an elegant sandwich.

"The little bookshop next door," she improvised

quickly. "I thought it might be nice to browse through it after lunch."

"I'll go along with that." He smiled. "But are you sure that's what was on your mind? I'm learning to read those jungle-cat eyes of yours, you know. I haven't worked out all the various expressions yet, but I'm getting there." He paused significantly and Savannah knew she wasn't going to like what came next. "I'm convinced that after I've made love to you, my sweet, you won't be able to prevaricate at all without me knowing it!"

"Cord!" Savannah gasped, nearly choking on her sandwich. "Don't you dare say things like that in public! Don't get the idea that simply because I'm allowing you to spend the day with me, I'll tolerate such behavior!" She scowled furiously at him, aware of the warmth in her face. It was extremely disconcerting to sit across the table from a man who had no inhibitions about making clear his desire. She was going to have to teach him a thing or two about basic gallantry!

"How many men," Cord asked curiously, "have you managed to terrify with that particularly ferocious frown and tone of voice? Poor Daly couldn't take it for more than one round last night. Did you ever let Painter have the sharp edge of your tongue?"

"You're being deliberately nasty," she announced regally. "I don't have to answer such questions!"

"I'm only trying to point out the advantages of having a lover who won't turn tail and run the moment you lose your temper." He chuckled. "Now stop glowering at me like that and eat your sandwich.

160

Perhaps that bookshop will have a new novel out in that adventure series about the neurotic secret agent who's always running around saving the world and being traumatized by his own actions!"

"Oh!" Savannah exclaimed with the unquenchable fervor of the addict. "Are you reading that series too?" Cord's less-than-appropriate remarks of a few minutes earlier were forgotten in a flash.

"Haven't missed one yet," Cord allowed proudly, wolfing down a large bite of European ham and cream cheese. "One of the best all-out heroes to come along in years."

"And the poor guy's so human!" Savannah chuckled. "I've been dying to find someone else who's reading the books, but no one else at the office seems to be into them."

"You never asked if I was interested," Cord pointed out reproachfully.

"Well, frankly, it never occurred to me," Savannah told him glibly. "If I'd even thought about it, I would have decided you were probably interested primarily in those endless engineering magazines you subscribe to!"

"I've seen you pick them up on occasion," he teased.

"Only to read the columns on personnel and management," she defended with a small laugh.

"I told you a short while ago that many of our tastes were compatible. When are you going to learn to trust me, Savannah?" Cord asked with a surprising touch of whimsy.

For an instant there was something so appealing

161

in those sea-deep eyes that Savannah had an impulse to reach across the table and touch her pursuer. Touch him with the magic of a fantasy sorceress who could tame the wildest and most dangerous of animals and men. Touch him and have him reduced at once to eating out of her hand, the gray-green eyes full of love and adoration. . . .

"Trust you, Cord?" she asked gently, sitting very still. "For a weekend?"

"Yes," he said, pouncing at once. "For a weekend."

At once the magic disappeared. Savannah refused to let her disappointment over his short-term interest show, instead she summoned all her courage and, leaning forward with a dazzling smile, looked him right in the eye. "Go," she advised kindly, "to hell."

"Darling," he said smiling back, equally brilliantly, "you're so romantic!"

The bookshop, fortunately, provided exactly the setting for the change of conversational topic Savannah felt was needed. Cord really was into adventure fiction as well as a great deal of other reading material, and the time slipped by peacefully enough in low-voiced discussions of authors, characters, and mutual discoveries. All in all, Savannah concluded as they prepared to leave some time later with paper sacks full of finds, a restful interlude in the reckless game she was playing.

"Why don't we dump this stuff at the inn and go for a walk on the beach," Cord suggested as they crossed a narrow, tree-lined street clogged with tourists. He glanced down at her and Savannah nodded, unable to make herself refuse, although some instinct warned that the beach might prove a vulnerable battleground. There was something about the primitive mystique of the sea that matched the primitive maleness in Cord, and she wasn't at all certain it would be wise to combine them.

Half an hour later, both wearing rolled-up jeans and Windbreakers, Savannah and Cord made their way down onto the sand and began following the edge of the pounding surf.

"Do you often go on vacation by yourself?" Cord asked after several moments of common silence. He had taken her hand, grasping her smaller fingers tightly within his, and now she was locked to his side in an unshakable grip. It was just as well she was as tall as she was and could manage to keep up with his long stride, Savannah decided in wry humor. Cord showed no interest in slowing his pace to match hers. He simply moved down the beach with the healthy, rangy movements of a large predator and expected her to stay with him.

"I have for the past few years, yes," she replied, wondering at the direction of the question. "Acapulco, Hawaii, a Caribbean cruise . . ."

"Such an independent little creature." He chuckled, slanting a look down at her. "You've been allowed to run wild for too long, I think," he added consideringly. "Or perhaps I should say, just long enough."

"Long enough for what?" she demanded spiritedly, not appreciating his superior manner.

"Long enough for me to find you," he clarified, eyes warming with meaning.

"You're certainly putting a lot of effort into obtaining one short weekend," she sniffed, her gaze focused firmly ahead on a group of gulls.

"You should know me well enough by now to know that I'm capable of putting a great deal of effort into getting something I want. And I do want you, my amazon." He stopped suddenly, pulling Savannah slightly off balance so that she stumbled and wound up in the circle of his arms.

"Cord," she began determinedly, her eyes lifted to meet his, her fingertips on his shoulders. "I don't—" She wasn't certain what she was going to say, she only knew she ought to be making some sort of protest.

"Hush," he whispered, holding her in the crook of one arm and lazily, tantalizingly, beginning to unzip Savannah's Windbreaker. His fingers slid across the material of the blouse underneath and she saw his eyes widen slightly as he felt the softness of her unconfined breasts.

"Don't you ever," he threatened half humorously but with a huskiness in his tone that conveyed a small threat, "let me catch you so improperly dressed on a beach with another man!"

Savannah, who had assumed that the layers of blouse and loose-fitting Windbreaker were more than sufficient for modesty, was stung into retorting. "You mean until after you get your weekend?"

"Are you hinting that you want more than a weekend with me?" he mused interestedly. "I'm amazed.

164

Here I thought it would take all my powers of persuasion just to collect the minimum debt!"

"Your ego could use a quick dip in that ocean!" Savannah snapped, embarrassment washing over her as he misunderstood her meaning. "What makes you think I'd want so much as a weekend with you!"

"Ah, well," he sighed, bending close, "I suppose I'll just have to settle for what I can get." His mouth suddenly covered hers, warm and sensually plundering. Savannah made one weak attempt to escape, but his hand, which had been only idly exploring the inside of her blouse, abruptly closed possessively over one breast, palming the nipple with a blatant urgency that acted like a leash on her, halting her efforts to break free. There was a warning in his kiss and the caress of his hand, a warning that said more clearly than words he could and would hold her as long as it pleased him.

"Why do you want to fight me when it's going to be so good between us, my sweet vixen? Like a little wild creature who's afraid to acknowledge how pleasant it can be to be stroked and petted. What's the matter, Savannah? Afraid you'll like it too much?" Cord muttered against her throat. "Let me show you. Let's find out if you will like it too much. Just relax and trust me long enough to demonstrate. . . ."

There was that compelling, hypnotic sensuality in his words again, Savannah thought despairingly. How did a woman fight this kind of seduction when her whole body yearned to let Cord sweep her into the waiting vortex of his passion?

"I won't have a weekend affair with you, Cord," she managed through tightly clenched teeth. "I'm sure you're every bit as good a lover as you seem to think, but there are other men in this world! Men who can offer me more than a couple of nights of sex!"

"I didn't *offer* you a weekend," he grated heavily, his hold tightening until her ribs ached. "I *won* it from you! You agreed to it and by heaven, you're going to pay off!"

Before she could respond, he had parted her lips again, seeking the inner warmth he seemed to crave, searching, stealing, claiming with such unstoppable authority that Savannah felt her self-control slipping farther and farther out of reach. Her body relaxed against his hardness, molding itself instinctively to his needs.

"Savannah," Cord breathed, his hands moving upward to frame her face as he lifted his head for a brief moment. "Someday I shall make love to you on a beach like this one. I swear it. You were made to respond to the most basic part of me and one day I must have that response; I will have it! Do you believe me?" The emerald fires in his eyes were only barely banked, Savannah realized with a curious exaltation. It would take so little to push him over the edge, to incite him into making good on his promise here and now.

But then what would she face? common sense intervened shrilly. Only the frightening prospect of an incredible regret. For she would never be quite the same person if she let Cord's brand of magic consume her totally. She must have her own sorcery waiting to ensnare him before she surrendered.

"Do you believe me, Savannah?" he demanded softly as she remained breathlessly silent. The fire in him flamed a little higher and she knew it would be safest to give him his answer.

"I believe," she temporized cautiously, "that you think you're going to do it. . . . Ouch!" she concluded on a small surprised shriek. He hadn't hurt her, not really, merely startled her with a small, impatient shake.

"Savannah," he threatened almost mildly, the passion fading from his expression to be replaced by a rueful determination. "I suggest you show a bit more faith in me than that or I'll make this the beach and today the day! And while the sand may be deserted at the moment, it is open to the public . . . !"

"Cord! You wouldn't do such a thing!" Savannah gulped, not in the least certain of him.

"Want to bet?" He grinned wickedly.

"Don't," she begged, "use that phrase with me again! Have you no compassion at all?"

"No," he growled, "only a fierce desire to hear you admit the truth. That I'm going to make you mine someday soon. Tell me you know that deep inside yourself. That it's only a matter of time before we stop playing this game!"

Savannah blinked, momentarily terrified by what he might have guessed. No, he was speaking of the game he had inaugurated, she realized in the next instant, relief flooding through her. Cord could know nothing of her own schemes.

Yes, she agreed bravely, "it's only a matter of time before we come to the end of the game." She faced him unflinchingly, noting the satisfaction in his eyes and wondering what his reaction would be if he knew just how intricate the game had become.

He smiled down at her with the charming smile of one who thinks he's obtained a major concession and can therefore afford to be generous. "That's it, Savannah, you'll find it will get easier now that you've acknowledged the final ending. But don't fret, honey, I'll still give you time." Folding her close against his side, Cord rezipped the Windbreaker, kissed her lightly on her upturned nose, and started back down the beach toward the inn. The complacency in him was overwhelmingly apparent, providing Savannah with exactly the spine-stiffening ingredient she needed at the moment. Cord Harding was not going to have everything his own way, she vowed silently. He was not going to emerge from this contest of wills as the sole winner!

"The day has slipped away, hasn't it?" he was noting as they approached the little inn. "Almost time for a sunset cocktail and then dinner. By the time we both shower and get the sand out from between our toes it will be almost six o'clock. I'll stop by your room and collect you about then, okay?" He wasn't exactly asking her permission, Savannah realized wryly. He was merely trying to be polite about implicit command.

"That will be fine," she agreed, thinking of the single red rose and the card that were due to be

168

delivered at six. The timing was going to be just about perfect . . . !

"Umm," he chuckled, pausing at the entrance to the inn to drop another quick, possessive kiss on her nose. "I like you when you're so delightfully agreeable!"

Savannah demurely dropped her gaze, hiding the gleam of expectant revenge she was afraid he might notice. "I imagine that's because you're accustomed to being the boss," she sighed.

"You're probably right," he surprised her by saying with a laugh. "It's been a long time since I took orders from anyone. Giving them gets to be a habit, I guess!"

Savannah dressed with care for the evening ahead. Brushing the dark pelt of her hair until it gleamed, she knotted it into a sophisticated chignon. She chose a dashing, off-the-shoulder black dress that fell in slinky folds to her ankles and paired it with black patent-leather sandals. Surveying herself in the full-length mirror, she reached for a crimson bead necklace and earrings to add a splash of exotic color. And then, her heart beginning to beat a little faster with a combination of nerves and excitement, she sat down on the edge of the bed to wait. It was a toss-up as to which would arrive first: the rose or Cord.

In the end they both arrived almost simultaneously. At the knock on her door Savannah rose, disliking the growing unease she was experiencing. What was the matter with her? Everything would go as planned and Cord would learn he had some competition. Wasn't that exactly what she wanted to achieve?

Nevertheless it was with a certain hesitation that Savannah opened her door.

"Hello, Cord," she began politely, not knowing whether to be relieved or anxious over the fact that he had arrived prior to the rose. "I'm almost ready."

"Good." He smiled with bland self-confidence. "I'll come in and wait." He pushed easily against the door and Savannah backed helplessly. This proprietary attitude of his was precisely why she was having that rose sent!

"Miss Emery?" A young man's voice from out in the hall interrupted the proceedings.

"Yes?" Savannah edged past Cord who turned curiously to watch the delivery person approach. There could be no doubt about the business the youth represented, Savannah thought, wanting to chuckle. He wore a shirt patterned with brilliant flowers and the name of the florist shop. In his hand he carried a long, narrow box elegantly wrapped in silver paper and a huge white bow.

"A package for you." He smiled cheerfully.

"Why, thank you," Savannah replied, giving him the benefit of her brightest smile in return. Reaching out, she accepted the box, her eyes following the young man as he retreated back down the stairs in great loping strides.

"What," Cord asked softly from the doorway, "is that?" He peered suspiciously at the rose box.

"You mean it's not a surprise from you?" Savannah managed lightly, carrying her prize triumphantly back into the room.

"No," he denied shortly, closing the door quite firmly behind them. He came to stand directly behind her, watching as Savannah fumbled with the ribbon. She sensed the growing disapproval in him and concealed an inner grin. So far, so good.

With the air of a woman anticipating a lovely present, she unwrapped the package. There was a tense silence from behind her as she finally lifted the lid.

"Oh!" she gasped, bringing all her acting talent into play. "How beautiful!" The dark red rose lay, as ordered, against a white satin backdrop. The epitome of romance.

"Who the hell sent you this?" Cord demanded, apparently untouched by the poetic event. He put a hand into the open box and grabbed the card before Savannah realized his intention.

"Give me that!" she ordered protestingly, clutching the box with one hand and making a swipe for the card.

"I want to see what fool thinks he can get away with sending you roses," Cord rasped, ripping open the tiny envelope and letting it fall to the floor.

Savannah watched in eager wariness as he scanned the brief message.

It was only as he raised flaming green eyes to meet hers that she first admitted silently she might have overplayed her hand. Seldom had she seen such tight-mouthed anger on a man's face. His veiled warning earlier about the extent of his temper came back to her.

She should have heeded that warning, Savannah decided with the clear vision of hindsight, because she was now facing a man who looked ready, willing, and able to beat her!

CHAPTER EIGHT

"Who—who sent it?" Savannah whispered, making an attempt to finish playing out her chosen role. In any event, it seemed safest to pretend innocence of any prior knowledge!

"Don't you know?" Cord growled, crushing the card in his hand with casual violence. "Are there so many men in your life at the moment that you can't imagine which would send you a single red rose?"

He took a step toward her and Savannah fell back under the impact of his tightly leashed anger. He was furious, she realized frantically. Far more furious than she had ever intended to make him, and the anger showed in every line of his tautly muscled frame.

"Cord, please," she tried placatingly even as she took another step in retreat. "You have no right to be so upset and you must know it. Who's the card from?"

"No right!" he snarled, ignoring her question. "What the hell do you mean, no right! You know damn good and well you belong to me! You have since the other night when I won you during that card game!"

"You didn't win *me!* " Savannah cried, outraged on one hand and frightened on the other. "You only won a—a weekend!"

"That's all I needed," he shot back, moving forward another menacing step. In a moment she would be up against the far wall with nowhere to run. He seemed content to close in slowly; a predator who knew the final outcome of the hunt and was going to tease the prey unmercifully with the knowledge. "One weekend with you will satisfy me completely and I'm going to have it, Savannah Emery, regardless of how many roses Jeff Painter sends you!"

"Jeff!" she gulped, trying to pretend astonishment. "Jeff sent the rose? He must have changed his mind —"

"I don't care how many times he changes his mind! He's had his chance and now it's my turn." Cord put out a hand and yanked the offending rose box from Savannah's shaking fingers. She watched, nervously chewing on her lower lip as he tossed box and contents into the nearby trash basket.

"Cord, this is ridiculous! It's only a rose!"

"Did you contact him, Savannah?" Cord demanded, gliding to a halt directly in front of her, both hands reaching out to grasp her shoulders. The cut

174

of the black dress exposed a great deal of vulnerable skin and Savannah wondered if Cord realized he was bruising her. He probably didn't care. "Answer me!"

"No!" she squeaked honestly enough, and the truth to that question, at least, must have been plain in her wide tawny eyes, because some of the grim lines at the corners of his hard mouth faded.

"Then how did he know where to send that rose?"

"How should I know? I suppose he could have found out where I was staying the same way you did! By asking one of my co-workers!"

"Well, you're not going to respond, is that understood? You're not going to call him or write him or see him . . . !"

"I—I should at least th-thank him," Savannah suggested tremulously, trying to read the depth of emotion in those narrowed green eyes. She'd achieved her goal, she thought sadly. Cord was displaying a fine sense of jealousy, but he still seemed concerned only with the weekend he had won! Where did that leave her?

"You'll do no such thing!"

"If—if he calls me—"

"I'll do the talking for you," Cord informed her arrogantly, giving her a short admonishing shake.

"I have my rights, Cord Harding, and I won't be intimidated by you!" Savannah grated, feeling goaded. The helpless feeling she had whenever he put his hands on her, whether in anger or in passion, was difficult to accept.

"Savannah," he threatened with unbelievable coolness, "if I catch you even attempting to contact

175

Painter, I swear you'll spend a month eating your meals off the top of my mantel, admiring the artwork we're going to find for the wall behind it!"

Savannah's golden eyes blinked once in astonishment. A month! He'd said a month! "You'd beat me?" she asked, more for something to say than anything else. Her mind was whirling with the implications of his threat. Had it just been a slip of the tongue for Cord or did he really mean to extend the relationship beyond a weekend?

"With the greatest pleasure, if I thought for one moment you were going to defy me in this business with Jeff Painter!" he assured her bluntly.

"Threatening me is hardly the way to make me agree to pay off my gambling debts," she pointed out acidly.

"I'm not so sure about that," he countered grimly. "Threats may be the only way to handle a stubborn, infuriating, willful little gambler who doesn't have sense enough to fold her hand and admit defeat! I've warned you about my lack of patience, Savannah!"

"You're reacting as if receiving the rose from Jeff was my fault," she complained with a touch of petulance.

"You seemed happy enough to get it!"

"I didn't know who'd sent it!"

"I'd already told you it wasn't from me," he snapped meaningfully.

"So what? Every woman loves roses!" she argued.

"Even from a man who has just abandoned her for another woman?" he bit out.

"Perhaps I find it flattering to know he's regretting

his actions," she suggested with a regal lift of her chin.

"I should think," Cord told her forcefully, "you'd be more interested in a man who knows what he wants right from the start. One who doesn't get side-tracked by the first cute ball of fluff who walks past!"

"Oh, I'll credit you with knowing what you want, Cord," she blazed. "It just so happens that it doesn't happen to coincide with what I want! How many times do I have to tell you I want more than the promise of a weekend with a man?"

"And how many times do I have to tell you that our relationship doesn't have to be limited to one weekend?" he rasped, his fingers digging into her soft skin, his face a hard, unyielding mask of sheer determination.

"But you just said a couple of minutes ago that a weekend was all you needed! It would satisfy you completely, you told me!" she wailed angrily.

The flaring green eyes still gleamed with the remnants of his fury, but a shuttered look slipped into place as he studied her glaring features. "A weekend," he stated evenly, almost cruelly, "would give me what I want. If you want more to exist between us, then it would be up to you to use the time to convince me."

"Me!" she yelped, astounded. "What are you talking about?" A nameless fear curled into life somewhere in the pit of her stomach. She had an awful premonition of what he was going to say next.

"Isn't it obvious?" he asked, one russet brow lifting coolly. "A weekend is what I gambled for and won. And I'm going to collect, Savannah, believe me. But," he added with unbelievable casualness, "there was nothing in our deal that prohibits you from using those two days and nights to play for higher stakes. . . ."

"What?" she shrieked, enraged and suddenly very much afraid. "I'm supposed to be lured into paying off my debt on the off chance I might be able to make you conceive a long-term passion for me in the space of two days?"

"Don't forget the two nights," he drawled, pulling her against the length of his body, one hand sliding down her spine to propel her intimately into the heat of his thighs. "A lot can happen in two nights once both parties cease hostilities."

Cord's lips found the sensitive place behind her ear, which was exposed by the neat chignon, and Savannah found herself staring in wide-eyed nervousness at the fine material of his evening jacket from a distance of about two inches. Her head was a chaos of emotions as she realized what was happening. Cord was offering her another way of playing her hand. A way that would prove far more risky than the method she had just tried. God! she thought feelingly, if he knew she'd deliberately set out to make him jealous . . . ! She wondered if his reaction would be anger over having been tricked or gloating over the knowledge that she wanted him enough to go to such lengths.

But why not another tactic? Oh, not precisely the one Cord was suggesting; that was too dangerous and everything was in his favor. Under his plan Cord would get his weekend and she would only get a small chance at something more meaningful. In fact, Savannah decided ruefully, he was probably hoping she'd pay her debt out of a false hope there would be more than a weekend involved. He was trying to manipulate her into getting exactly what he wanted.

What would happen if she softened her approach? Appeared to be on the verge of surrendering. Would some of the masculine aggression in him fade when it no longer fed off her challenge? And, more importantly, what would replace it?

"Cord," she began, pitching her voice to a gentler, placating level, "don't be angry with me. I won't contact Jeff." She tried for just the right touch of submission without sounding suspiciously meek.

"You'd better not! Put him and his damn rose out of your mind, Savannah. My weekend is your first priority." He tightened his hold on her, making her acutely aware of the feel of him as she found herself enfolded.

"You're undoubtedly one of the world's more tenacious men," she sighed, closing her eyes as his hand lingered on the curve of her hip. Then she murmured carefully, trying to keep the cool speculation out of her voice, "I can't believe any man would go to these lengths merely to collect on a bet he shouldn't have been so ungentlemanly as to make in the first place!"

"The fact that I *was* so unchivalrous should have warned you I'd be the type to collect," he retorted, lifting his head from the warm assault on the nape of her neck and fixing her with a warning glare.

"You've made your point over the matter of the rose and I've told you I won't contact Jeff so"— Savannah lowered her eyes to the button just below his white collar—"could we please go down to dinner?" she concluded wistfully, a little startled to hear just how gently pleading she sounded. She was a better actress than she would have suspected!

Cord set her slightly away from him, assessing her mood. A frown still lined his brow and the edges of his hard mouth, but the anger in him was rapidly disappearing. Savannah watched him through lowered lashes, telling herself to be careful not to overdo the dramatics and wishing that there wasn't quite so much reality in her tactics. The urge to placate and pacify this rather large man was genuine, she discovered with an inner wince. What's more, it was a new sensation for her. Her normal reaction to any man making the sort of scene Cord had just made would have been extreme impatience. Then again it was far from normal for her to deliberately contrive such a situation in the first place!

"Is this the beginning of sweet feminine submission?" Cord asked interestedly, surveying her new, unchallenging expression. She heard the edge of humor in his words and instantly a great deal of her desire to placate went up in smoke. "Are you really going to listen and obey?"

Gazing up at him with her most expressive, soulful gaze Savannah said in a tremulous voice, "I would do just about anything to get my dinner."

For an instant Cord stared at her and then he burst into rich laughter. "That's my Savannah! Always has

180

her priorities straight. Come along, honey, and I'll see to it your fires are properly refueled. I wouldn't want my woman to complain that I don't take proper care of her!" He swung her out of the room, the rose forgotten in the wastebasket by the bed.

The next couple of days were nerve-racking for Savannah, who found herself spending almost every waking moment in Cord's demanding company. Together they explored the antique and craft shops of nearby Monterey, drove along the scenic coastline, and spent hours walking on the beaches. Using the need to find Cord the artwork he wanted for his mantel as an excuse, they deliberated over one wall hanging after another. With a sense of increasing urgency, Savannah sought to take advantage of every discussion, every excursion to learn more about Cord and to force him to learn more about her. They must become friends before she could take the risk of letting them become lovers, Savannah told herself time and again.

For his part Cord seemed willing enough to comply with her efforts, no doubt seeing them as a way of getting her to drop her defenses. But no matter how much closer Savannah felt they had come to friendship during the day, his passionate, seductive good-night kisses left her with the impression that he was only biding his time, waiting for his weekend. It was that knowledge that made it possible for her to send him from her room two nights in a row.

"How many more nights are we going to spend apart?" he demanded huskily as he reluctantly prepared to take his leave the second night. He held her intimately against him and Savannah knew he was willing her to respond to the heat and desire he was making no effort to hide. The smoldering green gaze raked her determined face, noting the disarray of her hair, the vulnerability of lips he had softened with passion.

"Please, Cord," she whispered, using all her inner strength to stick to the battle plan. "It's such a big decision and I want to be sure. . . ." She let her voice trail off wistfully, her eyes wide and golden.

"There's no decision for you to make except that of choosing the time," he countered, one hand going to the zipper of her gown. The previous evening she had asked him to leave before he could do more than warm them both with his kisses. She had no intention of allowing him to get them on the seductive softness of a bed again as he had a few nights earlier.

"Cord, you promised you'd leave when I asked you to go," she reminded him carefully, aware of the opening zipper. "Last night you left. . . ."

"Last night I let you send me away too soon," he murmured, his fingers warm on the skin of her back. His mouth tracked kisses down her throat to the fine bones of her shoulder. "I was trying to show you how cooperative I can be," he added laconically. "But after I got back to my own room, I realized I'd handled the situation all wrong. Gave you a little too much power. I've told you, you're a lot like me, little amazon; give either of us power and we'll exercise it!"

"That's not it at all!" she protested thickly, feeling the tremors shoot through her as his hand slid along the smoothness of her skin just inside the open dress. "Can't you understand? A woman has to be sure!"

"Sure of what?" he asked, easing the bodice of the gown forward and tightening his hold as she stiffened momentarily in response to his action. "Sure that you can control me? Sure that our weekend will be on your terms? If that's what you're holding out for, Savannah, forget it. I'm using all the self-control I possess now just to let you choose the moment of your surrender, but once you've committed yourself, I'm going to collect my winnings on my own terms. For the space of a weekend, honey, you're going to know what it's like to belong completely to me."

"Is collecting on this bet all you can think of?" she cried into the fine material of his shirt. She had been longing to hear him reassure her, to talk in some detail about a future together. She had spent the last two days doing everything in her power to search out common interests and establish a basis for real relationship, and still all he talked about was that damn weekend!

"It's the most important thing on my agenda at the moment," he informed her wryly, starting to move her gently across the room toward the bed.

Savannah felt the purposefulness in his body and knew he was intent on a major seduction assault, one she wasn't at all certain she had the power to resist. She stifled her panic and tried to speak firmly.

"It's time for you to go, Cord." She waited tensely in anticipation of his possible refusal.

"You don't mean that, Savannah. You've sent me away too many times and regretted it afterward."

it's only your ego that likes to think I've regretted it," she retorted, digging in her heels so that he came to a stop. "I'm perfectly content to keep sending you away until I've made up my mind about how I feel!"

"I'll help you make up your mind," he promised. "Don't be such a coward, sweet Savannah, it isn't like you. Why are you so afraid of me?"

She wanted to laugh a little hysterically at the honest lack of understanding in him. "I'm not afraid of you. But that doesn't mean I'm prepared to leap into bed with you, either," she said fiercely. "Now please leave, Cord. You're making things very difficult for me."

"I'm doing my best to make things easy for you," he corrected, beginning to frown. "You're being obstinate, honey, because you're afraid of what will happen after we've spent a night together. That's it, isn't it?" he demanded. "You're terrified you'll really lose yourself to me!" He looked so certain of his deduction that Savannah wanted to strike him.

"That's not true!" she managed, barely containing her rising temper. "Please, Cord. I need a little more time." It took all her self-control to put that touch of earnest pleading back into her voice. It would have been far more satisfying to simply tell him to go to hell. But feminine instinct warned that this man wouldn't back down under a verbal attack. Besides, it was important to give her current game plan a fair chance and that meant maintaining the appearance of being close to surrender. If it didn't work, she vowed silently, she would try something else. "You're still a stranger to me in many ways," she went on gently. "Can't you understand that?"

"Only because I'm not like the other men you've been seeing," he told her kindly, his fingers kneading the sensitive area at the nape of her neck. "But that's no reason to be frightened of me. I swear you won't regret our weekend. I'll make it good for you, Savannah. You *know* I can do that. You must realize by now that we've got something special between us, and we owe it to ourselves to explore it."

"You mean you think I owe it to you because of that stupid card game!"

"Yes!" he growled, his patience clearly close to exhaustion.

Savannah quickly regained her composure. "You may be right," she breathed, wishing he could see something special between them that encompassed more than the physical and would satisfy more than his desire for conquest. "I don't know. Give me a few more days, Cord. I won't make you wait forever." She tacked that last sentence on in a hurry as his mouth tightened ominously.

"No, I won't allow you to make us wait much longer," he retorted grimly. "Sometimes I think the best way to handle this is to simply change my mind about letting you decide the time and place. I'm beginning to think it was a mistake letting you have that much power."

"No, Cord," she protested quickly, becoming very uneasy at the speculative gleam in his eyes. "I—I appreciate your consideration. Please don't change

185

your mind." How ridiculous to be thanking him for not pressing immediately for demands he had no right to make in the first place, Savannah thought, fuming silently. Still, she didn't want to risk invoking his temper while she was in such a delicate situation. Better to maintain the gentle, pleading facade for now. "Just a little while longer, Cord?"

"How much longer, Savannah?" he asked tautly, the thumb of his left hand tracing the line of her jaw in a considering fashion that alarmed her. "One day? Two?"

"I—I was thinking more in terms of a couple of weeks or so . . ." she began hesitantly.

"The hell you were!" he snapped, the anger in him igniting visibly. "You're out of your mind! If that's the way you're thinking, you can forget it. I have no intention of spending my entire vacation alone in my own bed. I'm here for a reason, Savannah Emery, and don't you forget it!"

She didn't dare respond aloud to his small explosion of frustration and impatience. There was too great a chance that anything she said would merely serve to fan the flames. Instead Savannah stood very still, unconsciously chewing on her lower lip, watching him with all the female supplication she could put into her expression.

Cord took a deep breath and Savannah waited anxiously for his response. To her vast relief he relaxed with a suddenness that was confusing. His hands dropped from her as if from a heated surface and he stood looking down at her broodingly.

"All right, Savannah," he finally sighed after a

186

tense moment. "A little more time. Are you very, very sure this is what you want?"

"Yes." She barely got the small word out of her dry throat.

"I warn you," he went on with a sort of repressed violence as he strode over to a nearby chair and recovered his jacket, "I don't intend to let this situation drag on indefinitely." He adjusted his loosened tie with a quick, masculine gesture that conveyed his frustration more clearly than words.

"Cord," Savannah reminded him daringly as he made for the door, "you're the one who told me you knew where you'd gone wrong in handling me. You said yourself I needed the right to make the decision. . . ." She followed him from a safe distance, halting as he turned to face her, his hand on the doorknob.

"I'm doing my best to treat you with kid gloves, Savannah," he told her tightly. "But I have my limits. After all, you owe me the two days and two nights. It's not as if I were making unfair demands! And you should know by now that patience isn't one of my more shining virtues!"

"Have you any at all?" she couldn't resist interjecting, seeing that he was halfway out the door.

"Oh, yes," he shot back blandly. "I persevere in the face of discouragement and I always make certain to collect what's owed me. Two traits that have gotten me where I am today!"

"Where, exactly, is that?" she challenged, tawny eyes narrowing slightly.

"The position of being your boss!" With that parting comment he was gone, leaving Savannah to swallow her retort.

With a strong sense of foreboding she went about the ritual of preparing for bed, her mind whirling with plans and a growing sense that time was running out. Damn that man! she thought bleakly, sliding between the cool sheets and tugging the blanket up to her chin. Couldn't he focus on something else besides his precious weekend? What was she going to do if she couldn't make him see beyond the business of collecting his winnings? Run away again? That was beginning to look like the only alternative. Would he pursue? Savannah grimly watched the flicker of shadows on the wall across the room and decided he very well might come after her if she tried another disappearing act. Cord had been quite right when he declared that perseverance was one of his strong points. But even he must have his limits. How far would any man chase a woman when all he wanted from her was a lousy weekend?

On the other hand, Savannah told herself determinedly, what if the problem was Cord's well-known single-mindedness? He had homed in on the weekend he felt was owed him and nothing else would be allowed to get in the way. If he got his weekend, what would happen then? Savannah shivered. She was rationalizing again, looking for a reason to surrender to a man she should be ignoring completely. But wasn't there some hope in the fact that Cord wanted her so intensely, even if it was only for a weekend? Surely he wouldn't have made the bet in the first place unless he was attracted to her. . . .

With a muffled groan Savannah plumped her pillow and told herself to go to sleep. In the morning she would think of something else to try. This business of pretending to be on the verge of paying her gambling debt wasn't working very well at all. She would have to come up with another tactic.

But all the various schemes and plans that came to mind at odd moments during the night came to an untidy jumble the next morning when, after dressing for breakfast and an early morning walk on the beach, she found herself pacing the room, wondering why Cord wasn't knocking on her door.

Had he had second thoughts? Had her refusal to comply with his demands pushed his patience too far? She glanced at her watch, grimacing ruefully as she acknowledged the fact that she missed his proprietary knock and his possessive morning kiss. No doubt about it, Savannah decided gloomily, she was the one who was weakening in this nerve-wrenching game!

Well, she told herself gamely as time crept past, she wasn't going to stay in her room until Cord chose to collect her like a piece of baggage! Slinging the strap of her purse over her shoulder, Savannah yanked open the door and stepped out into the hall—only to come at once to a stunned halt.

There was another woman in the hall and she was standing in the doorway of Cord's room, her long-nailed hands wrapped around his neck. For a painful second Savannah simply stared, her key dangling from her fingers, as the tiny silvery blonde stood delicately on tiptoe to plant a quick, butterfly kiss on Cord's cheek. His hands were at her small waist.

"I'll meet you at breakfast, darling," the blond creature whispered. "Just give me a few minutes to unpack, will you? These early-morning flights are a strain, aren't they? But when Ella told me you were in Carmel vacationing, I didn't waste a second getting here. We're going to have such fun!"

To Savannah's unbelieving eyes the other woman looked like a bright, beautiful insect as she patted Cord's tanned face and darted lightly away to disappear into the room beyond his.

Savannah's first instinct was to go after the stranger and haul her out of the hotel by the scruff of her dainty little neck. The wave of possessive savagery was frightening in its intensity. Her second impulse was to confront Cord, preferably with unsheathed nails, and demand an explanation. But in the last crucial instant the saving grace of not wanting to make a scene came to Savannah's rescue. Her final, dominant reaction was to try and get out of sight before Cord turned and saw her.

But she wasn't fated to be so lucky. Even as she reinserted the key in the lock, Cord glanced ever so casually in her direction, one red brow arching immediately in interested inquiry. The hard line of his mouth gave away nothing of his thoughts.

"Why, good morning, Savannah. Come to fetch me for breakfast?" he asked cheerily, leaning one arm against the doorframe as the slow feral smile slashed into place across his face. He was dressed in slacks and a partially buttoned shirt, which exposed too much masculine chest, as far as Savannah was concerned, and his still-damp hair was lightly ruffled as if someone had just stroked it with long-nailed fingers.

There was nothing for her but to brazen out the situation, Savannah realized immediately. She forced a cool expression. "Not if you have other plans," she assured him sweetly, flicking a glance significantly down the hall.

"Oh, you mean Irene?" he responded innocently. "Yes, she'll undoubtedly be joining us. She's a rather persistent little thing, I'm discovering." He appeared vaguely concerned over that, and Savannah could have screamed.

"Then you won't be needing my company," she stated, abruptly aware that her hands were shaking. She swung around on her heel and marched regally toward the stairs, half hoping and half terrified that he would call her back. When he didn't, she was left to wonder if it was because he had no intention of explaining the situation or if he simply didn't want to risk waking other guests by yelling down the hall.

With every intention of storming out of the inn and finding herself another place to have breakfast, Savannah found she was striding briskly toward the hotel dining room and justified the action by declaring silently that she would not let the other woman upset her plans. With a fine sense of hauteur she took a seat at a table for two, the smallest she could locate, and ordered coffee.

She was lacing the dark brew liberally with cream when she sensed Cord's presence in the room. Instantly every nerve and muscle tightened in response and she wondered if she was doomed to go through life with such a primitive reaction to one man. Deliberately she refused to glance behind her and watch his approach but she could feel him as he closed the distance between them.

"You certainly were in a rush this morning, weren't you?" he noted, sliding into the seat opposite and reaching casually for her discarded menu. "Couldn't wait to get the caffeine into your bloodstream?"

"I didn't want to interfere with your morning plans," Savannah declared, hating his cool manner.

"Aren't you even curious about Irene?" he inquired lightly, signaling the waiter for coffee. He studied Savannah's remote expression with slightly narrowed eyes. There was a speculative, waiting look about him that made her very nervous.

"Curious?" Savannah echoed icily. "Why, no. I just assumed she was a—er—close friend of yours." She realized she was stirring her coffee with undue vigor and made herself relax.

"How astute of you," he mocked. "She is, indeed, an acquaintance of mine. Her parents own the farm next to Aunt Ella's. You remember Aunt Ella? The person I was talking to on the phone the night you showed the more cowardly side of your nature?"

"Must we go through that again?" Savannah hissed tartly.

"Not if you'd rather discuss something else," he offered at once.

192

"Go on," she ordered grimly, wanting to use her knife on his throat.

"Let me see, where was I? Oh, yes, Aunt Ella's neighbors. They're the Pattons, and Irene is their daughter. She is also," Cord added laconically, "something of an embarrassment for me."

"A previous lover who won't let you alone?" Savannah hazarded scathingly. She could feel herself seething and had all she could do to maintain her composure.

"Not quite," he smiled coolly. "A potential lover who won't let me alone would be a more accurate description, I'm afraid. You see, Irene recently broke off her latest engagement—her third I believe—and she's decided I'm next on her list of prospective husbands. She's been hounding Aunt Ella to have me come for a visit to the farm or to otherwise arrange a casual reunion. My poor aunt has about reached the end of her patience. She doesn't want to offend the Pattons or hurt sweet little Irene and she doesn't want to continue playing bodyguard for me. Apparently she gave up the defense entirely and told Irene I was staying here in Carmel. Serves me right, I suppose, but just the same, I don't think I'll leave word with my answering service the next time I take off for a vacation!"

"Let me get this straight," Savannah muttered in disbelief, staring at him. "You're being pursued by the daughter of your aunt's neighbors? And you don't want to encourage her? She—she seemed quite attractive. . . ."

"She is but she carries a high price tag," Cord

retorted bluntly. "Marriage. Even I wouldn't risk Ella's wrath by having an affair with the daughter of her best friends!"

Savannah whitened. She knew she shouldn't be so shocked to hear him declare his lack of honorable intentions toward the opposite sex, but still, it nearly unnerved her. She'd been building such dreams! A slow anger began to seep into her bloodstream.

"I see," she said with what she thought amazing calm. "And you're not interested in marriage . . . ?"

"Not when I'm looking forward to my weekend with you," he returned coolly, glancing up as the waiter approached.

Savannah's hands clenched into fists under the table. How could she have let herself fall in love with this man? "Your aunt had the right idea," she grated feelingly. "You should be made to deal with the situation."

"Left to my own devices, I shall undoubtedly wind up hurting or offending everyone concerned: the Pattons, Ella, and Irene," he vowed. "My solution will be to tell Irene to get lost. She'll be hurt, her parents offended, and Ella will be furious with my lack of diplomacy."

"You do have a problem, don't you?" Savannah snapped.

"One you can help me with, honey," he stated smoothly just before he turned to order his coffee.

"Me! What am I supposed to do?" she gasped as the waiter disappeared.

"You," he told her blankly, "are in the perfect position to discourage Irene."

"I don't understand," Savannah whispered, stunned.

"Think about it," he ordered softly, his hard features giving away nothing of his thoughts. "All you have to do is make it clear you're the current woman in my life and that you intend to stay current for some time."

"Why should I do you any favors?" Savannah barely got out between suddenly dry lips. She sat very still, watching him with wide, incredulous eyes.

"Because," he said, smiling dangerously, "I'm in a position to do you one."

Savannah blinked, beginning to feel quite trapped by the mesmerizing effect of the cold green eyes pinning her. "What are you proposing?" she demanded in a low voice.

Cord leaned forward intently, everything about him hard and dominant. "I'll let you have another chance with Painter if you help me out of this mess."

"What!"

"You heard me," he growled. "Do me this favor and I'll let you respond to his damn rose!"

CHAPTER NINE

"You're asking me to pretend to be your mistress!" Savannah could hardly believe what she was hearing. The slow anger began building into a fine rage. "This must be very important to you" was all she could say, her eyes dropping instinctively to hide her expression. She had, it seemed, gained nothing during the past few days. Pressured by a conniving young woman who wanted marriage, Cord was more than willing to surrender his claim on Savannah.

"It is," he confirmed darkly. She could sense his will reaching out for her.

Savannah knew she should get up and walk out of the restaurant, leaving Cord to his dilemma. Indeed her white knuckles were tightened in anticipation of bolting from the chair. And then the tension was broken by the sound of a woman's voice.

"Sorry to keep you waiting, darling. Did you order

197

me a cup of coffee?" Irene swirled to a halt beside the table, her lovely hazel eyes flicking with cool apprais-al over a silent Savannah. "And who is this, Cord?" she asked with a false, bright charm as he politely got to his feet and located a third chair. "A friend you've met here in the hotel?"

The word "friend" was uttered with such subtle sarcasm that Savannah's temper threatened to slip the leash entirely. Did Cord really expect her to play the role of his mistress in front of this creature? Even if Savannah had been willing, she doubted that it would have worked. Irene clearly had enough self-confidence to handle a dozen mistresses.

"Irene, meet Savannah Emery," Cord said in a bleak tone as the blonde seated herself. His eyes were drilling into Savannah, willing her to go along with the role he was about to assign her. She could feel the sheer intensity of his dominance, and her own femi-nine anger rose even higher to meet it. "Savannah is"—Cord hesitated fractionally—"more than a friend."

"I quite understand," Irene smiled loftily, and her superior attitude finally pushed Savannah over the brink. So Cord wanted to be rescued from the mar-riage-bound clutches of this she-insect, did he? Well, Savannah would save him. Her way!

"Do you?" she smiled with saccharin sweetness in response to Irene's comment. "I'm so glad. You can be the first to congratulate us!" Savannah wasn't aware. that in that moment her normally laughing smile was every bit as dangerous as Cord's feral grin. She ignored him as he resumed his seat, her attention

198

focused politely on the attractive young woman who had materialized as a rival. But even though she wasn't watching him, Savannah could feel Cord stiffen warily across the table.

"Congratulations! Whatever for?" Some of the charming friendliness vanished from Irene's pretty face.

"Cord!" Savannah admonished with seeming amusement. "Didn't you tell her?" She waited, glorying in her small power as the tension in him heightened. He was uncertain of her now, beginning to wonder what sort of monster he had created, no doubt. But Cordell Harding was an old hand at the poker-faced strategy of a game-playing management meeting, and he rose to the occasion with what Savannah felt was commendable ability.

"No, honey," he drawled, and only Savannah saw the warning glitter deep in the emerald eyes. "I'll let you do the honors."

"What's going on?" Irene demanded petulantly, her narrowing gaze swiveling between the other two.

"Cord and I were planning to announce our engagement when we returned from this trip," Savannah explained, dropping her small bombshell with a surging rush of revenge. "I thought you realized . . . ?" She let the sentence trail off, as if she were too polite to imply the other woman wasn't very observant.

"Your engagement!" Irene nearly shrieked. "That's impossible! I don't believe you!"

"Ask Cord," Savannah suggested coolly, covering a sudden small nervous dread by taking a sip of coffee. Over the rim of the cup her eyes met his, and she would have given a fortune to know exactly what he was thinking. But perhaps it was better not to know, she decided grimly. Now it was up to him. How badly did he want rescue?

"Is this true, Cord? Are you really engaged to—to this person?" Irene hissed quickly, struggling to regain her composure.

"Yes," Cord said simply, his eyes never leaving Savannah's. "I'm going to marry her."

He was going to go along with it! Savannah could hardly believe it. He must have wanted to be free of the annoying problem of handling Irene enough to submit to Savannah's small revenge. It wasn't much, she told herself drearily, but there would be some pleasure in watching Cord pretend to be engaged to her in front of Irene Patton.

"Well, I must say this is a tremendous surprise! Your aunt certainly knows nothing of this!" Irene added accusingly, her eyes on Cord's hard face.

"She was going to be the first to know until you showed up so unexpectedly," Cord declared smoothly, further surprising Savannah with his acting ability.

"When are you going to be married?" Irene demanded, a note of suspicion in her voice.

Savannah stepped in to answer that one, not quite trusting Cord to come up with an appropriate response. "We haven't set the date for certain, but it will be in the near future, won't it, Cord?"

"Oh, yes," he confirmed dryly. "The very near future. Savannah and I are far too much in love to wait very long, for the legal side of things," he told Irene kindly.

Irene shook her head in clear disbelief. "I can hardly believe this. You've given no indication of being in love with anyone. . . ."

Cord chuckled at that, the gleaming green eyes going to Savannah's now wary expression. "Shall I tell you just how much in love with Savannah I am?" he asked Irene lightly. "She," he stated with the air of one making an astounding announcement, "has driven the Mercedes!"

Savannah frowned, not understanding, but it was obvious the statement had an impact on Irene.

"You let her drive it?" The small blonde looked surprisingly crushed.

"Not only did she drive it, she managed to put a scratch on it," Cord went on grandly. "And I'm still engaged to her!"

Savannah felt the red creeping into her high cheekbones. It was clear the damn Mercedes was a more valued possession than she had realized. Irene looked positively stunned by the revelation. The other woman bravely summoned a smile.

"Privileged, indeed," Irene noted wryly. "Cord hasn't let another soul behind the wheel of that car since he got it a few months ago. I'd have thought he would have murdered anyone who actually scratched it!" she added with just a hint of spite.

"I didn't even beat her." Cord grinned. "Although I won't say I wasn't sorely tempted! True love, wouldn't you say, Irene?"

"Cord, honey, you should have told me how much

you valued the car," Savannah murmured, goaded. "Perhaps I would have found other means of transportation on that particular occasion!" She glared at him through lowered lashes.

"You were in such a hurry, as I recall, that I didn't have the heart to refuse permission. Besides," Cord went on, an edge to his words that only Savannah heard, "you asked so nicely and you know you can wrap me around your little finger!"

Savannah nearly choked on her coffee.

"How did you two meet?" Irene injected a bit stiffly, clearly making an effort to remain superficially polite.

"Savannah works for me," Cord explained easily.

"*Worked* for him," Savannah couldn't resist clarifying.

"Oh? You're going to give up your job now that you've managed to land a successful man?" Irene asked rudely.

"I don't think it's a good idea to work for one's husband, do you?" Savannah retorted lightly, ignoring Cord's abruptly disapproving expression. She couldn't tell whether he was annoyed at her or Irene. "But I wouldn't think of quitting work altogether. No," she went on with a certain relish, "I plan to accept a position with Cameron Engineering." Deliberately she manufactured a job with Cord's chief rival and smiled brilliantly as it became his turn to nearly choke on the coffee.

"The hell you will," he informed her with an equally brilliant smile.

"You'd rather she didn't work?" Irene pounced

202

sympathetically, apparently grasping what she mistakenly saw as an opportunity to drive a small wedge.

"I don't mind her working but I can guarantee it won't be for William Cameron!" Cord stated, speaking directly to Savannah, whose smile continued to mock him. In spite of the gloomy outlook for the game in which they were competing, this latest twist was proving almost amusing.

"But, darling, you've just told me I can wrap you around my little finger, so I wouldn't make any rash statements if I were you," she purred.

"Do all fiancées set out to see how far they can push their prospective husbands?" Cord asked, as if vitally interested in a curious social phenomenon.

"I wouldn't know," Savannah demurred politely. "Why don't you ask Irene? Weren't you telling me she's been engaged a number of times?"

"What!" There was an audible gasp of outrage from Irene's side of the table, and Savannah took another measure of satisfaction from having caused it. "Cord! How could you?" the other woman wailed, the hazel eyes moistening suspiciously.

"Savannah's—uh—twisted my words, Irene," he said quickly, reassuringly. "You know I understand about your previous engagements."

"I always thought you did," Irene whispered in a low, hurt tone, gazing soulfully at Cord's impatient expression. "You always seemed to understand about those others. They weren't important, Cord, you know that. I was only testing my wings, as you used to advise me to do. . . ."

203

"How sweet," Savannah murmured, smiling impartially at the other two. "A brother-sister relationship. I suppose that developed during the times you visited your aunt on her farm, Cord?"

"Our relationship was hardly that of a brother and a sister," Irene informed her hastily, angrily. "Cord and I have been very close in"—she paused dramatically—"other ways."

"A father-daughter relationship, perhaps?" Savannah suggested helpfully, deciding the other woman was probably around twenty-three. Across the table she saw Cord wince visibly.

"Hardly!" Irene nearly yelped furiously. She was clearly about to continue when Cord interrupted a little desperately.

"I think we had better get breakfast ordered or the waiter is going to lose all interest in this table," he stated firmly, including both women in the implied command. "What will you have, Irene?"

"Just a cup of coffee and perhaps some fruit. I'm really not very hungry," Irene said, sounding wistful.

"Fine," Cord said encouragingly, fixing Savannah with a determined expression. "The usual for you, sweetheart?" The words were polite enough, but Savannah knew that if she said anything wrong just then she would find the menu wrapped around her neck.

"That will be fine, darling," she agreed submissively, her tawny eyes mirroring her inner laughter.

Breakfast became a balancing act as Irene utilized every opportunity to emphasize her previous mysterious relationship with Cord, and Savannah responded by treating the little blonde as a pesky insect who would soon be out of the way. Cord, caught in the middle, was making every effort to maintain a web of polite social fiction around the table. His attempts to pacify Irene and control Savannah's increasingly outrageous remarks were vastly amusing to his supposed fiancée who wondered if he'd guessed what he was getting into when he'd asked her to help him out with his problem.

"How long will you be staying, Irene?" Cord asked, apparently reaching for something uncontroversial.

"I—I don't know," Irene said uncertainly with an appealing look. "I had thought we could have some time together, but—"

"But she's much too sensitive to want to intrude on a newly engaged couple, I'm sure," Savannah concluded cheerfully. "I'll tell you what, Irene, why don't you check into the matter of a return flight for yourself and then Cord and I can drive you to the airport?"

Irene glared at her, but said nothing until the meal was finished and she stood beside Savannah in the lobby, waiting for Cord to fetch his jacket from his room. As soon as he had disappeared in the direction of the stairs with what Savannah considered temporary cowardice, the blonde whirled on her.

"You're not going to get away with this!" Irene hissed furiously. "He's no fool, and it won't take him long to see you're nothing but a money-grasping hussy. He may be happy enough to sleep with you for a while, but he'll never marry you!"

"You sound very certain of that," Savannah noted coolly, watching her opponent through narrowed eyes. With Cord out of the room the gloves were off on both sides.

"I am!" Irene vowed. "He's just leading you on, I expect, letting you think you're going to marry him so that he can get what he wants from you without a lot of persuasion!"

"Really?" Savannah drawled dangerously. "Does he usually have to do that to get a woman to sleep with him?"

Irene flushed angrily. "I imagine he takes the easiest route to his goal!"

"Does that route often include buying the victim an engagement ring?"

"You're not wearing a ring!" Irene blazed triumphantly.

"Oh, there you are, Cord," Savannah announced as he approached somewhat warily. "Irene was just noticing my lack of a ring and I was about to tell her that finding one was on the agenda for today. Do you think we should invite her to join us while we look for one?"

To give the devil his due, Savannah acknowledged privately, Cord rallied strongly to the latest challenge. Something unreadable flickered deep in the emerald eyes and then he was smiling with patent intimacy into Savannah's upturned face.

"Why, honey, I've always thought of that as something to be shared just by the engaged couple, but I suppose if you really want the advice of another

206

woman . . . ?" He waited, russet brow cocked questioningly, for her decision.

"I'd rather just the two of us looked for it, but she's your friend and I didn't want to be rude," Savannah smiled charmingly, glancing at a fuming Irene.

"Do you mind, Irene?" Cord asked politely. "We could arrange to meet you later for lunch if you like."

"You're actually going to buy her a ring?" Irene looked startled, and Savannah wondered what fantasies she had been building about Cord.

"Of course," he stated airily, taking Savannah's hand possessively. "I rather fancy my woman wearing a traditional symbol of bondage. I guess I'm a bit old-fashioned in some respects," he added self-deprecatingly, ignoring Savannah's outraged gasp. "We might as well get started," he went on conversationally, leading his mock-fiancée off with an iron grip. "We'll meet you back here for lunch, Irene. Why don't you try a walk on the beach? Too cold for swimming, but the walk is invigorating." With a casual wave in the direction of the upset blonde, Cord hauled Savannah through the inn door and out onto the street.

"Whew!" he growled irritably as they stepped out onto the tree-lined sidewalk. "I don't know whether to be flattered or appalled at the way you moved in to 'rescue' me! Do you always assume your roles with such enthusiasm?"

"Serves you right for trying to palm me off as your mistress," Savannah declared breezily, actually having to hurry in order to avoid being dragged down the street. "What's the rush? We've got a perfect excuse to avoid your charming neighbor at least until lunch."

"At which time she will be looking forward with great anticipation to viewing an engagement ring!" he reminded her grimly, not slackening his pace. There was a set look to his face that made Savannah swallow with a hint of uncertainty.

"Details, details," she grumbled. "I'll think of some logical reason why we couldn't find one."

"There aren't any excuses. You're going to be wearing a ring come lunch or Irene will be hot on the scent. I know her, remember. She's already suspicious of your newfound status! Stop dragging your feet, Savannah," he added impatiently, giving her wrist a small yank. "You started this; you can damn well finish it!"

"But, Cord," she protested, "I don't want a ring. We'll only have to return it later and it's not as if we're really engaged. . . ."

"You should have thought of that before you elevated yourself from mistress to future wife!"

A long time later Savannah was still grumbling when Cord, apparently nearing the end of his patience, announced they were going to take a walk on the beach, one which he stated he hoped would exhaust her to the point where she wouldn't have the energy to nag him any further.

"I'm *not* nagging!" she snapped, conscious of the weight of the beautiful new diamond ring on her finger. "I'm just pointing out that I don't appreciate being used!"

"Who's using whom?" he shot back, leading her out onto the sand toward a cluster of rocky tide pools not far from the inn. "I'm the one who should be complaining. It's not every day a man's mistress declares she's going to marry him!"

"I'm not your mistress! Furthermore I don't intend to be your mistress. Not even for the damn weekend you keep demanding!"

"Don't give me that," he advised, grinning with sudden wickedness. "We both know I've almost got my weekend in the palm of my hand." Cord stopped his aggressive forward stride and pulled them both to a halt. "Admit it, Savannah," he ordered softly, cupping her stormy face with rough gentleness. "Tell me the truth, my amazon. I want to hear you acknowledge it!"

"I wouldn't give you that satisfaction," she gritted, stepping away from him with a stiff, resentful movement.

It was then that she spotted Irene standing on the short cliff above them. The other woman was watching them, the jacket of her expensive pantsuit blowing in the brisk sea breeze. There was a kind of avid curiosity in Irene's face that alerted Savannah. With sudden inspiration she turned back to Cord.

"Kiss me," she ordered, stepping into his arms. "Irene is watching."

"With pleasure," Cord agreed huskily, his hands closing on her at once. Before she could change her mind, Savannah was pinned tightly against him. "I trust you do know what you're doing, Savannah Emery," he grated just before his mouth took hers prisoner.

Savannah, not at all certain she understood her own actions, gave in to the temptation of the moment. It was wonderful to be able to enjoy Cord's fierce magic. She could almost have found it in her heart to thank Irene for the excuse. And that, she decided as her lips softened willingly under Cord's, was the way she would play the game. As long as Irene was anywhere in the vicinity. After all, Savannah told herself determinedly, she might as well get what she could out of the bizarre situation.

"Tonight, Savannah?" Cord whispered persuasively, his mouth moving hungrily along the path to her delicate earlobe. "Shall we begin our weekend tonight? Say yes, sweetheart, I know you want it as much as I do!" His hands tightened, pressing her firmly against the warmth of his body, and she thought she felt him tremble slightly.

"You forget," she got out in a desperate little voice, knowing she mustn't let Irene's presence drive her that far, "I'm only doing this to get you out of an embarrassing situation! I have no intention of actually giving you your weekend."

"No?" he asked gently, his mouth moving back to hover just above hers. There was mocking satisfaction in his eyes as he gazed down into her face.

"No?" You—you said . . ." she told him a little frantically, "you promised me a reward for helping you. You said I could contact Jeff. . . . Cord!" she concluded on a tiny shriek as his grip on her became abruptly painful. "You're hurting me!"

"You're lucky I'm not doing severe damage," he gritted between clenched teeth. "Haven't you enough sense to know better than to talk about one man while standing in the arms of another?"

"You're the one who was so anxious to escape sweet Irene that you promised me another chance with Jeff!" she defended herself hurriedly. "I—I won't bring him up as long as you don't bring up the subject of your stupid weekend!"

He studied her harshly for a long moment and then uttered a resigned sigh. "You are the most stubborn, annoying, difficult female I have ever met, do you realize that, Savannah?" Cord threw an arm around her shoulders and began walking across the beach toward the waiting Irene. "You're going to push me too far one of these days, you know that, don't you?"

"You've got a lot of nerve accusing me of being difficult . . . !" Savannah began explosively but was unable to continue her tirade as Irene came running lightly forward to meet them, her eyes on Cord.

"There you are. I was beginning to think you'd forgotten about lunch," she exclaimed brightly, ignoring Savannah.

"Not a chance. Savannah and I share, among other things, a keen interest in food," Cord announced dryly.

"Yes." Irene smiled sweetly at Savannah. "I did notice you ate a man-size breakfast this morning, Savannah. You want to watch that, you know. Cord likes his women slender. Oh, I see you got the ring."

211

Savannah obligingly held up her hand for Irene's quick, cursory inspection.

"Very nice," Irene said dismissingly as the three of them began walking back toward the inn. "Remember how you once told me you thought diamonds were so cold, Cord?"

Savannah glanced, startled, up at Cord's unreadable expression. He had been the one who had chosen the diamond she now wore.

"I don't recall saying that, Irene," he returned smoothly, "but in any case it's a good stone for Savannah. Fire and ice!" His arm tightened around her shoulders, and Savannah obligingly stepped closer. In spite of her irritation there was a sense of safety to be found close to his hard body. Safety from Irene and, in a strange way, from the future.

Enjoying that sensation and reveling in the many small attentions Cord showered on her in front of Irene, Savannah lost herself thoroughly in the new game of pretending to be engaged to Cordell Harding. For the rest of the afternoon she played the role of a woman in love with a man who returned her affection. There was a definite satisfaction in watching Irene grow increasingly frustrated with the situation, and by evening Savannah was certain the blonde would not be hanging around much longer. In a way she would be sad to see her rival leave, for with Irene gone Savannah would no longer have the excuse to play the game.

"Have you decided yet how long you'll be staying?" Cord asked conversationally after dinner as he escorted Irene and Savannah into the lounge. He glanced inquisitively at the younger woman.

"I expect I'll take off in the morning," she answered slowly, shooting a withering glance at Savannah, who pretended not to notice. "I think I'll visit some friends in Santa Cruz and then fly up to San Francisco. Robert is there, you know, and he's been trying to talk me into renewing our engagement." She paused a moment to see if that had any effect on her audience, but Cord merely nodded politely.

"He seemed the nicest of the lot." Cord pulled out a chair for Savannah.

Irene quickly masked a disappointed frown and became quite chatty, using her previous association with Cord to try and create an intimacy calculated to leave Savannah out of the conversation.

But Savannah was equally determined not to allow that to occur. Periodically throughout the evening she deliberately met Cord's eyes across the table with a warm, promising glance designed to effect the intimacy between herself and Cord that Irene was struggling to build. And Cord responded to it with satisfying enthusiasm. He would smile back at her with a sort of hungry male intention that Savannah had never seen in another man's face. It made her feel desired, as if she were the only woman in the room, and if it also made her feel hunted, she determined to ignore that aspect. It was having the result of shutting Irene out of the relationship and that was the only thing that mattered.

"Dance with me, Cord," Savannah ordered in a

soft, husky voice at one point, sensing that Irene was about to make the same request.

Without a word he got to his feet and led her out onto the floor, where she floated happily in his arms. He said little, but she sensed tension in the way he held her against him and wondered briefly at its cause. Didn't he realize she had almost completely put Irene out of the picture? By the time Savannah was finished tonight, the other woman would be packing her bags. A pleasant thought. When Cord reseated her back at the table, she let her hand linger invitingly on his arm, knowing Irene was watching in silent fury. Cord squeezed her fingers in response, letting his hand rest over hers.

"I didn't think you liked clinging women, Cord," Irene observed spitefully, her eyes on the small gesture.

"There is an exception in every man's life." Cord grinned, settling closer to Savannah. "With this particular woman the trick is getting her to cling tightly enough to satisfy me!"

Savannah met his wicked glance with her wide, laughing smile, enjoying a sense of female power. It couldn't last, of course; this was all a charade for Irene's benefit, and as soon as the other woman left, Savannah would have to go back to putting a careful distance between herself and Cord. But for tonight

· · ·

It was late by the time Savannah finally decided to bring the evening to a conclusion. Her younger rival had been almost completely routed and there was only one step left to finish off the image of a couple madly in love.

"Do you mind if we call the evening to a halt, darling?" she asked demurely, glancing at Cord from beneath her lashes. "I'm ready for bed," she added with a hint of soft meaning.

"Not at all," Cord returned smoothly. "Will you excuse us, Irene?" He rose politely and helped Savannah to her feet.

"I'll go upstairs with you," Irene said at once, a deliberate look in her eyes that said more clearly than words what she was thinking.

She wonders if I sleep with Cord, Savannah thought, planning her next move. After all, Irene had found Cord alone that morning. Well, the conclusion of tonight's little game should squelch any notions Irene might have been entertaining about a late-night visit to Cord's room.

Savannah's room was the first to be reached at the top of the stairs and she glided to a halt beside it, turning politely toward Irene but maintaining a proprietary hold on Cord's arm. A hold he didn't seem to mind in the least.

"Shall we be seeing you at breakfast in the morning or will you be trying for an earlier start to Santa Cruz, Irene?" Savannah asked brightly.

Irene's glance went to the hand on Cord's sleeve. "I haven't decided for certain yet," she responded coolly.

"Well, we might be rising a bit late, so don't wait for us," Savannah advised kindly. "After all, we're on vacation and not sticking to any particular schedule. Here's the key, darling," she added, digging it out of her purse and handing it to Cord. She accompanied the action with an inviting smile and wanted to laugh at the flicker of surprise she saw in the narrowed green eyes. He opened the door and with a curious glance handed her back the key.

With a last, superior smile for Irene, Savannah slipped her hand into Cord's, feeling his fingers twine instantly around hers, and, as if she had done it many times before, led Cord into her room. She had a brief glimpse of Irene's frustrated, angry expression as the door closed gently.

"I think you're safe for the evening," Savannah began humorously, dropping Cord's hand immediately and turning back to press her ear against the door. "She's going back to her room. I'll bet you never realized what a first-class actress I am, did you? Perhaps I should look into something else besides personnel work when I get back to Costa Mesa." She straightened from her position at the door and turned to smile at him. The smile faded rapidly into the beginnings of a frown as she realized Cord had crossed the room and was casually removing his tie.

"Don't get too comfortable," she remarked caustically, the frown deepening. "It will be safe for you to go back to your room in a few minutes. Just be sure you move around quietly so Irene doesn't hear you."

"You sound as if you've organized this sort of scene before." Cord smiled with a degree of affectionate amusement that made Savannah unaccountably nervous.

"I'm only doing what you've asked me to do," she pointed out righteously as Cord shrugged out of his jacket and slung it over the chair. "I—I was doing you a favor. . . ."

"No, Savannah," he corrected in a low voice that held no humor. "You went far beyond what I asked of you." There was something threateningly masculine in the way he began to unbutton the cuffs of his white silk shirt. Savannah bit her lip apprehensively. It dawned on her that she was going to have to be very careful how she concluded tonight's strategy.

"Cord," she began determinedly, "don't get any ideas about staying here!" She stood very still, her hands behind her, bracing herself against the door.

"No more games, honey," he announced a little roughly as he finished his cuffs and began opening the front of his shirt.

"Games!" she gasped, wondering once again if he had somehow guessed her various ploys. "But I'm not playing games, Cord!"

"You've been playing them all day, Savannah," he said, the corner of his mouth quirking upward as he watched her taut expression. His hands dropped from the last button and he started forward with such purposefulness that Savannah knew this time he meant to finish what he started. "And tonight you're going to find out how such games end."

CHAPTER TEN

"Did you enjoy playing the role of my future wife, Savannah?" Cord asked interestedly as he advanced. "Personally I rather enjoyed it. You seemed quite possessive, honey, but I imagine you would be that sort of wife."

Savannah edged away from the door, along the wall. She was going to have to get control of the situation quickly. Her mouth was dry, and she instinctively moistened her lips with the tip of her tongue. "Cord, you have no right—"

"In fact," he went on, changing direction slightly to follow her movement, "you seemed to slip very easily into the part of wife-to-be. As easily as you slip into my arms when you stop fighting me."

"Cord, this is very unfair of you," Savannah breathed, putting the chair between them with a swift little jump. She hated being on the defensive like this. The role of predator came naturally to Cordell Harding, but the role of being the prey was not to her taste.

"Unfair?" he retorted in a tone of mock outrage. "You're the one who's being unfair. Shall I count the many ways?"

"Name one!" she challenged bravely, wishing suddenly that Cord would either cease his stalking or grab her and get the unpleasant business over. Her nerves were strung so tightly, she thought they would snap. He was doing this intentionally, she guessed with rising anger. He was making her thoroughly aware of the primitive side of his nature as if he wanted her to experience genuine female helplessness.

"Where shall I begin?" he asked rhetorically, almost but not quite touching her as he circled the chair and trapped her against the side of the bed. "First, of course, we have the instance of your initial welching on our bet."

"Don't you dare bring that up again!" He was so close. Savannah considered the merits of scrambling across the bed to the other side. She would have to move quickly.

"Then we have the theft of my new car. . . ."

"Cord!"

"Shall we move on to the way you've continued to renege on our bet? Even though I've been so generous in allowing you to choose the time and place of settling it."

"Generous!" she yelped protestingly, glaring up at him and wishing she wasn't so painfully aware of the curling hair on his broad chest or the sexy warm male scent of him. "You told me I could see other men and then you changed your mind after I'd only had a couple of evenings out! Hardly generous!"

"So I underestimated my own fortitude." He shrugged dismissingly, his hands resting casually on his narrow hips. "Let's see, what happened next? Oh, yes, the rose and the slushy note from a man who has no right to contact you at all. And you seemed to enjoy getting both!" he added accusingly.

"I told you," she began heatedly, only to be silenced by a warning flick of his hand.

"Then we come to the matter of the way you've been teasing me," he went on inexorably.

"No," she gulped, swallowing her guilt. "I never meant to do that!" But she had, and the knowledge doubled her nervousness. She tried to cover the reaction with an intense frown.

"Perhaps you don't choose to call it teasing, but I do. All day long I've been subjected to the looks, the touch, the small demands of a woman in love, and that, my sweet Savannah, is what finally pushed me too far. It wasn't your stubbornness or your sharp tongue as I had expected. It was you pretending to be devotedly in love that finally did it. You made one too many promises with those big golden eyes, and tonight I'm going to collect."

"No!" Savannah hissed, belatedly trying to make a mad dash across the bed. But it was too late. With deceptively swift ease Cord reached out and grasped her wrist, yanking her gently against the hard planes of his chest. Her fingers splayed automatically across his shoulders as she sought for balance. She couldn't look away from the gleaming green eyes.

Desperately she pushed against him, struggling to compose a coherent argument in her head at the same time. It was enormously difficult to think under the tension of the moment. Relentlessly his arms closed around her, pressing her intimately against his thighs. Savannah could feel the fire that was smoldering in him, saw it in the darkening glance above her and felt her poor arguments dissolve beneath the impact of his undisguised desire. Still, pride demanded some effort.

"What about your promise?" she whispered tightly, pleadingly. "The one you made when you asked for my help this morning!"

"I don't seem to remember any promises," he murmured, gazing into her eyes as if into pools he was about to enter.

"Don't say that! You know what I'm talking about! You said if I helped you stay clear of Irene you would let me have another chance with Jeff!"

"Oh, that promise," he drawled, sliding one hand sensuously up her spine.

"Yes!"

"That was made on the premise that you were going to pretend to be my mistress. I consider it canceled the moment you told Irene we were engaged."

"Dammit! You can't do this to me!" Savannah wailed helplessly, shivering at the knowing stroke of his hand.

"In any event," he went on intently, his fingers

222

holding her at the vulnerable nape of her neck, "perhaps after a couple of nights in my bed you won't find Painter so attractive."

With the swift, shattering impact of a diving hawk Cord's mouth seized Savannah's, ripping through her weak defenses with contemptuous ease. Before she could even brace herself, he had parted her lips, arrogantly exploring her warmth and making it his. She trembled in his hold and he reacted by tightening it further until she could not move without somehow welding herself more thoroughly to his hard length.

"Cord!" she gasped despairingly as his lips freed hers to track the sensitive path to her earlobe. "I will not be your mistress!"

"No," he agreed with surprising grimness, swinging her suddenly off her feet and into his arms. "You'll be my mate. A mistress is a coy little thing who plays the part of amusing toy as long as it suits her. Tonight you're going to find out what it means to belong completely to me. There won't be any nonsense about being something as superficial as a mistress!"

He settled her lightly on the bed, following heavily and pinning her wrists above her head when she made one more desperate attempt to wriggle away. Deliberately his free hand went to the buttons of her silky blouse, his eyes never leaving hers as he slowly undid them. By the time he had finished the sensuous action Savannah was trembling beneath his touch.

"Talk to me, Savannah," he ordered in a dark, velvety voice as he trailed his fingers along the softness of her skin just inside the open edge of her blouse, pausing to undue the front clasp of her lacy bra. "Talk to me as if you really were going to marry me! I want to hear the words of love and need from you."

"Oh, Cord!" she managed breathlessly as he exposed her pink-tipped breast and bent to kiss it with gentleness. "What is it you want of me? Only tonight?"

"I want my weekend," he grated passionately, his tongue flicking across her nipple until it hardened in desire. "I want the two nights and two days you lost to me in that game of cards, my sweet amazon. And during that time I want everything from you that you have to give a man!" He slid the material of the blouse and bra away from her other breast and cupped its heaviness in his hand, letting his finger stroke the tip until Savannah thought she would go mad.

"And—and what will you give me in return?" she whispered huskily, her legs moving with restless need until he shifted his weight to anchor her more firmly. He was lying half on top of her now, letting her feel the strength in him.

"You can have whatever you are strong enough and brave enough to take," he rasped thickly, loosening his grip on her wrists long enough to pull the blouse completely free of her body. With an unconsciously savage gesture he hurled it into a shadowy corner of the room and then went to work on the remainder of her clothes.

In the space of a few moments Savannah lay completely naked on the bed, watching as Cord removed his own clothes with impatient urgency. He was so beautiful, she thought suddenly, her eyes beginning to reflect the rising hunger she sensed deep within herself. Uncompromisingly male and capable of making her blindingly aware of her own femininity. He had said she could have whatever she had the courage to take from him. . . .

Shivering in need and apprehension, Savannah put her arms around Cord's neck as he finished undressing and moved back down beside her. She was stunned to feel him tremble at her touch. Quite suddenly she felt herself grow vastly more brave. Her head tipped back across his arm, she gazed up into the lambent green flames of his eyes.

"A woman like me wants more from a man than a night or two of lust," she warned him in a soft, throbbing tone.

"Is that so?" he growled, shifting abruptly to cover her entire body with his. His gaze was only inches from her own. "What does she want?" He let his weight crush her into the bedclothes until she knew she could never escape, even had she wanted to try. His hands framed her face, his thumbs playing possessively with the line of her jaw.

"She wants as much as she can get," Savannah murmured, her fingers twining deeply into the thick reddness of his hair. "She—I—I want love and passion and honesty. . . ."

"You want to chain me to your side?" he clarified, baring his teeth in a grin of primitive male laughter.

"Yes!" she almost snarled, enraged by his amusement. Her fingers tugged fiercely on his hair, and her

225

body arched angrily against his. "You can't take everything from me and not give me everything in return!" she swore, knowing even as she made the vow that he could do anything he liked in that moment.

"I told you," he reminded her, using his greater strength to master her struggles, "you're free to try and take anything you want!" He bent his head and traced a fiery row of kisses along her throat down to a point between her breasts. "Show me how much you want me, my amazon!" he commanded hoarsely.

Savannah reacted to the naked male desire in him as if to a potent drug. Her own anger and passion and fierce need combined to form a source of strength she would never have guessed she possessed, and she wielded it with feminine intuition.

But no matter how much she fought him for the embrace or struggled to control the lovemaking, Cord was always one step ahead of her, using his own power to chain and dominate and control her until at some point she realized vaguely she was responding to his touch, his demands, as if he were the source of her strength, not its target.

"I want you," she admitted on a mere thread of sound as his hands explored and possessed the most intimate parts of her body.

"And I want you," he said huskily. "I've wanted you for so long that I can hardly bear to wait any longer." His mouth closed hot and passionately demanding over hers once more.

Savannah felt the tremors coursing through his lean, hard frame and stroked his smoothly muscled back with the tips of her nails, glorying in his response.

"Tell me you belong to me, Savannah," Cord grated harshly, wrenching his mouth free. "Tell me that tonight you'll pay off the damn debt without any reservations, without holding anything back!"

Savannah opened her eyes to meet the flaming demand in his and heard herself whisper softly, invitingly, "Yes, Cord. Tonight I belong to you." Silently she added fiercely to herself, *And you belong to me. It may only last for a night or two, but I will take what I can get!*

With a low sound of masculine need and triumph Cord parted her legs with his own, sliding possessively into the final embrace with a heat and fire that made Savannah cry out softly in a feminine surrender that was also designed to be a trap for the male of the species. A trap every woman held buried deep within herself, waiting for the right man to spring it and be caught inside.

Savannah felt her strength unite with Cord's as he guided them both to a dizzying height and then jumped with her over the edge in an exultant defiance of everything else in the world except themselves.

The aftereffects of the blaze died away slowly, leaving Savannah coiled in Cord's arms, listening to the sound of his heart. They were both damp with perspiration and exhausted as if they had run a great distance.

"It was better than I had dreamed it would be, Savannah," Cord murmured into her hair with deep satisfaction. "Tell me it was right for you too. Don't lie to me. Not now."

"It was perfect, Cord. The most exciting, thrilling thing that's ever happened to me," she told him with absolute honesty and felt the pleased response of his body.

"Good," he whispered, sounding suddenly sleepy. "Go to sleep, sweetheart. In the morning we'll talk." She sensed him drifting off into a deep slumber and wondered what was to become of her now.

Savannah dozed fitfully, awakening once a couple of hours later to find Cord, propped on his elbow, gazing down at her in the darkness, his fingers trailing lazily over her skin.

Seeing her eyes flutter open in mute question, he smiled and dropped a languid kiss on her breast. "I couldn't wait until morning," he told her, half apologetically, half aggressively. "I haven't gotten used to having such a treasure buried in my bed within easy reach!" He made love to her again, this time with a slow, erotic grace that elicited soft sounds from the back of Savannah's throat. Sounds that seemed to please Cord inordinately.

The next time Savannah awakened, there was a grayness in the room that told her dawn was not far off. With the grayness came the harsh edges of returning reality.

Turning her head, she watched Cord sleeping, loving the sleep-induced vulnerability she would never have guessed existed in him. He was everything she had ever wanted in a man, including a great deal more that she hadn't suspected she wanted until he had taken her captive. *My God!* she thought with appalled sadness, *how will I go on living without him?*

Sooner or later she would discover the answer to that awful question, Savannah told herself grimly. Because Cord had offered her nothing more than the promise of an affair. An affair that might last no longer than a few days. If she had come to feel like this toward him in such a short period of time, how would she feel if she hung around until he grew tired of her? Clinging to him through a future that had to be lived day by day was suddenly the most frightening thought Savannah had ever had.

Better to end matters swiftly, common sense shouted silently in her brain. She was a strong woman but she wasn't at all certain she had the fortitude to survive being Cord's mistress. In spite of all the passion that had flowed between them last night, there had been no talk of love or permanency.

Feeling cold and abandoned, even though Cord still slept beside her, Savannah sat up slowly in bed, trying to decide what to do next. Only one emotion seemed to offer any strength in that moment. The emotion of anger.

Deliberately Savannah fanned a smoldering unhappiness with her future lot into a female fury that brought with it a strange warmth and determination. It was all Cord's fault, she decided with suddenly acute reasoning. From the moment he had stepped into her world by involving her in that stupid card game until last night, when he had let her know in no uncertain terms that she would never be completely satisfied with any other man, he had pushed, prodded, and herded her into this disaster. It was all his fault, and she could do nothing to punish him for it!

Bitterly Savannah edged out of bed, careful not to disturb the sleeping red lion. She badly wanted a shower but didn't dare take one for fear of waking him. The important thing now was to get away, and Savannah focused all her rising, angry energy on that goal. She would not stay to be the mistress of a man who had so cavalierly stolen her heart and didn't seem particularly interested in giving his in return. Surely if he had felt some love for her, Cord would have made it plain last night!

Shivering in the chilly room, Savannah slid into her jeans and pulled on a velour sweater. She couldn't take time to pack. Cord might awaken at any second. Instead she grabbed her purse, which contained the essentials of a woman's life, and started for the door.

Only to stop short as she realized how difficult it was going to be to get out of town at this hour. She had turned in the rental car the first day she had arrived and by the time she could arrange for another, Cord would undoubtedly be awake and looking for her.

Then she spotted the keys Cord had absently dumped on the chair last night as he was undressing. The keys to his rental car. Without giving the matter further thought, Savannah picked them up, careful not to let them jangle, and headed once again for the door, letting herself stealthily out into the hall.

There was a horrible sense of loss as she descended

the stairs in the quiet, sleeping inn and passed through the lobby. She had a brief, fleeting thought about paying for her room but decided Cord could handle that. It was little enough repayment for what he had done to her!

It was difficult to keep her anger at a high enough pitch to provide her with the determination she needed not to turn around and run back to her room, but Savannah managed it by keeping the bleak prospect of her future with Cord constantly in front of her eyes. Eyes that were blurring suspiciously as she trailed through the inn's tiny parking lot, trying to remember where Cord had parked the car.

Eventually she found it and had to wipe the moisture from her cheeks as she leaned down to unlock the door. Then she was inside, twisting the key ferociously in the ignition. Throwing an arm over the back of the seat, she turned to glance out the rear window before backing out of the narrow space—and blanched at the sight of Cord striding mercilessly toward the vehicle.

His harsh features were set in a cold, threatening anger that made Savannah's temper seem tame by comparison. He moved so quickly that he was beside the driver's door before she could get the shift lever into reverse. The window was open.

"Give me the keys, Savannah," he snarled, leaning down and meeting her eyes brutally. "Right now!" he barked when she hesitated, eyeing him wordlessly.

Unthinkingly she responded, removing the keys from the ignition and, with shaking fingers, dropping them into his outstretched hand.

"All right, out of my car," he instructed, wrenching open the door with ill-concealed fury.

Savannah glared up at him, beginning to know real fear. She fought the weakening emotion with her only weapon: anger.

"Don't you dare give me orders, Cord Harding," she blazed. "After what you've done to me, the way you've treated me, you have no right to tell me to do anything!"

"You can either get out of that car by yourself or I'll drag you out! Take your choice!"

Seeing no immediate alternative, Savannah climbed out of the car, vaguely surprised to find her knees held.

"You've got nerve, woman, I'll give you that!" Cord allowed between clenched teeth as he slipped the car keys into his pocket. He was wearing the slacks and shirt he had worn last night. He hadn't taken time to rebutton the shirt and it flapped lightly in the cold dawn breeze. "Just where in hell did you think you were going?" he snapped, reaching out to take hold of her shoulders as she stood before him.

Savannah drew a deep breath, trying to decide how to answer his question. Never had she seen a man so flamingly angry. Everything they had ever claimed about a redhead's temper was true apparently. The gray-green eyes glittered with terrifying intensity, and the whiteness around the edges of his mouth testified to his barely restrained emotion. But Savannah had emotions of her own that were barely restrained.

"Where do you think I was going?" she lashed out bravely. "I was trying to get away from you!"

"How many times did you think I'd let you run from me?" he bellowed, his fingers flexing painfully into the skin of her shoulders. "What does it take to teach you that you belong to me, Savannah Emery? Shall I beat you? Will that do it? Believe me, I won't hesitate for a moment if that's what it will take to control you! I've been so damn patient with you and what do I get in return? Lies and tricks!"

"It's only what you deserve for the way you've hunted me down like some sort of—of animal!" she shrieked, uncaring about the possibility of waking a few guests in the rooms above them. "Well, you had your victory last night and I hope you enjoyed the conquest because it's the last time you'll ever have that opportunity!"

"Oh, no, it's not!" he raged back at her, shaking her roughly as if she were a kitten. "You're mine now, you damn vixen, and I'll take you as often as I like! And what's more, you'll respond just like you did last night! You can't resist what we have between us, and one of these days you'll admit the truth! I swear to God I'll chain you to my bed until you do! I won't give you another chance to run away from me!"

"You can't stop me!" she hissed, infuriated. Her tawny eyes showered golden sparks as she faced him with all her courage, her fists clenched tightly at her sides.

"Want to bet?" he invited menacingly, hauling her closer.

In spite of herself Savannah winced at the pointed reminder of how she had got into this situation. She blinked but refused to say anything.

"I'll do anything I have to in order to tame you to my hand, Savannah. And it will be my hand and no other man's you'll respond to, little tigress! I'll·get rid of any other male who comes within your orbit as easily as I got rid of Painter and Eric Daly. . . ."

"Jeff!" she gasped, startled. "What are you talking about?" A tiny flicker of hope stirred somewhere. "You didn't deliberately—"

"Send Painter to the San Diego office?" he concluded bluntly. "You better believe that's exactly what I did! As soon as I realized you were going to concentrate on him as long as he was anywhere in the vicinity! I wanted the competition out of sight and out of mind. But he didn't quite make it out of your mind, did he, Savannah? I was planning the next phase of my campaign when he very conveniently did what I expected him to do and took up with another woman. He's a weak man and I figured it wouldn't take long. What was so damn frustrating was that you persisted in being the loyal type!"

"You deliberately disrupted my romance with Jeff?" she breathed, shocked.

"Yes." He nodded aggressively. "And I came to the party that night knowing just what sort of mood you'd be indulging!"

"How could you have known?" she whispered, not knowing whether to scream at him or cry.

"I knew because, as I've told you before, you're a lot like me, Savannah. In that position I would have

234

been more than a little interested in revenge, and who better to take it out on than the person responsible for removing your intended victim from the picture?" Cord's eyes gleamed with remembered satisfaction. "It was easy enough to maneuver you into that card game and let you think you were unbeatable until I had you agreeing to the bet I wanted!"

"You mean you planned on making me wager a whole weekend of my life?" she asked, unable to comprehend exactly what was happening but knowing she had to get to the bottom of this or have no peace of mind at all.

He grinned savagely, shaking his head once. "No, you crazy female. I was only going for dinner and a kiss. I figured it would give me the opening I needed to start making you aware of me. I couldn't believe my own good luck when I was able to push you into that weekend. I fully expected you to reject that particular wager!"

"You cheated!" Savannah hissed.

"For all I was worth," he confirmed with unrepentant arrogance.

"Of all the low-down, sneaky, underhanded things to do!" she blazed. "Well, it won't do you any good, Cord. I won't be your mistress, do you hear me? I refuse!"

"Why?" he demanded at once, his face close to hers as he held her still in front of him. "Tell me why not!" There was a new, ragged edge to his voice.

"My God!" she breathed, incensed with his lack of perception. "Don't you know by now? Can't you guess? I don't want just a weekend or even a week

235

or two with you!" She saw his face harden and added with incredible recklessness, "I want a lifetime with you and you aren't prepared to offer me that! Don't you understand, Cord?" she yelled at him. "I love you!"

For an instant there was an amazing stillness in the turbulent atmosphere flaring between them. And then, with awesome abruptness, the anger drained from Cord's face and something else took its place. Something that combined laughter and relief and masculine delight.

"You love me!" he echoed, giving her another, gentler, shake that managed to send her hair flying. "You *love* me! Damnation, woman, why didn't you tell me!"

"Why should I tell you?" she bit out brashly, uncertain of his mood. "You'd only have used the knowledge against me to get your damn weekend!"

"You're right about that," he agreed, chuckling. "I would have used any weapon that came to hand!" he added with great depth of feeling. The green seas of his eyes flowed over her, drinking in her belligerent, tense expression. "Don't you realize why that weekend meant so much to me, you little idiot?"

"Why?" she asked helplessly, hardly daring to breath.

"Because I was going to use it to make you so thoroughly mine that you wouldn't be able to say no when I told you we were going to be married!"

"Married!" It was Savannah's turn to be incredulous. "Cord, are you saying you wanted to marry me all along? That you love me?"

"So much so that I would have moved heaven and earth to get you, my sweet amazon!" he growled fiercely, pushing her face into his shoulder as he pinned her tightly against him. Savannah didn't mind. She was too happy to be concerned about minor details like breathing.

"Oh, Cord," she whispered delightedly. There was moisture in her eyes again, but this time it was caused by joy. "Why didn't you say anything? Let me know how you felt? I thought all you wanted was a weekend. The novelty of collecting on a foolish bet just to satisfy your ego."

"You didn't love me in the beginning, Savannah," he reminded her gently, cradling her against him and shielding her from the chilly breeze with his warm body. "Your mind was still involved with Painter and what you might have had with him. I had to find a way to make you look at me and realize I was the right man for you. I kept thinking that if I could only get you—" He broke off suddenly and Savannah giggled at the ruefulness in his voice.

"Yes, Cord?" she prompted, leaning back against his arm to fix him with a fond look.

"I kept thinking that if I could only get you into bed," he said determinedly, enjoying her blush, "everything would be clarified. I decided a weekend of learning how much I needed you and how you needed me would be sufficient."

"You kept saying all you wanted was a weekend," she said wistfully.

"At the end of which I was going to have you so thoroughly weakened that you'd go along very meekly with the idea of marrying me," he retorted. "I should have known that meekness simply isn't one of your prime character traits!"

"No, but I've discovered that game-playing is," she told him cheekily. "While you've been pursuing your goals, Cord, I've been going after mine! I was going to make you see me as something more than a weekend fling. Why do you think I encouraged Eric Daly?"

"To make me jealous?" he guessed, the line of his mouth hardening slightly.

Savannah nodded, as unrepentant as he had been earlier. "And then there was the rose and the note from Jeff. I had them sent to myself, Cord."

"I will beat you, after all!" he declared ferociously. "You came very close to disaster with that little gambit," he added dangerously. "Don't ever, ever use another man to manipulate me again, do you hear me?"

"Yes, Cord," Savannah agreed submissively, her eyes dancing.

"You won't need to resort to that tactic, anyway," he went on wryly. "Just continue to love me, Savannah, and I'll be completely at your mercy!"

"Cord, about Irene . . ." Savannah began delicately.

"What about her? I thought I made it clear from the beginning I'm not interested in Irene!"

"I know, but you were willing to let me go back to Jeff just to keep from getting involved with her. . . ."

"More scheming on my part," he confessed with

a sigh. "I was getting a little desperate, and when she showed up, it seemed the perfect opportunity to embroil you even more deeply in my life. I had some notion that if you started playing the role of my woman, you'd actually begin to see yourself living it for real! I sure as hell didn't intend to let you go back to Painter."

"But, as usual, I was ahead of you," Savannah told him with her wide, warm, laughing smile. "I wanted to play the part of wife, not mistress!"

"And I liked you so well in the role that I decided to find out what it was going to be like being your husband!" he grinned back. "Marry me, Savannah!" he ordered, holding her close.

"Whenever you say," she whispered contentedly.

"As soon as we can get a license, then," he told her forcefully.

"What's the rush?" she asked, thinking of the remainder of the vacation in Carmel.

"It's my responsibility to do what I can to prevent you from pursuing your new line of work," he informed her, lowering his head to take her lips.

"What new line of work?" she demanded just before he kissed her.

"Car theft."

"You think you can rehabilitate me?" she murmured a few moments later when he had temporarily freed her mouth.

"It will be my life's work," he chuckled. "After all, I'm the one who started you off on your life of crime. Maintaining eternal vigilance over your behavior is the least I can do to protect society!"

"I had no idea you were so concerned with protecting society." Savannah grinned admiringly. "I've always thought of you as a man who lived pretty much by his own rules and let society take care of itself."

"Yes, but in this particular instance my own interests are at stake. I have to find some way of protecting my means of transportation," Cord sighed, wrapping an arm around her waist and guiding her back toward the warmth of the inn.

"Cord," Savannah began carefully, wanting to make a point, "I'm really not a bad driver. I wasn't the one who put the scratch on your car that night. . . ."

"That's all right," he assured her magnanimously. "You can make up for it on your wedding night." He bent his red head to drop an arrogant, possessive little kiss on Savannah's ruefully wrinkled nose. "You owe me a lot, don't you, sweetheart? I'm looking forward to spending the rest of my life collecting."

Three nights later Savannah slipped happily into her new husband's arms and prepared to give herself up to the pleasures of dancing with Cord Harding. She closed her eyes, her head settling contentedly against his shoulder, and made a small sound of satisfaction as the music began.

"Happy, Mrs. Harding?" Cord asked softly, his hands holding her warmly close.

"Very happy, Mr. Harding." She smiled. "And you?"

"Funny you should ask." Savannah felt the laughter deep in his chest. "I've never been happier in my life. Nor," he added meaningfully, "have I ever known a greater sense of relief than I did this afternoon when we finally put the last of the relatives on a plane and shipped them out of Carmel!"

Savannah giggled, remembering the little scene. "If I ever had any questions about how you became so successful in the business world," she declared, "they're all answered now. You've displayed a pure genius for organization during the past three days. Imagine arranging that lovely little ceremony in the chapel by the sea, lining up a minister, taking care of the blood tests—" Savannah broke off momentarily to gaze with delight at the gold ring on her left hand.

"What you were witnessing were the actions of a truly desperate man!" Cord informed her feelingly, holding her closer. "Never have I been so stunned as I was to have Aunt Ella arrive here within hours after I'd safely packed sweet Irene off!"

"She's a charming person, Cord. I enjoyed her enormously," Savannah interrupted impulsively.

"So do I but not when she took the bit between her teeth and began arranging *my* wedding!"

"Well, she felt she was your only relative, and it was only natural she wanted to attend."

"I suppose once she was on the scene it was inevitable that your parents had to be contacted at once," Cord sighed. "I just didn't expect them to show up that night. You never told me they live in San Francisco. Good Lord, it was only a short jaunt down here for them!"

"They certainly took to you and Aunt Ella both," Savannah pointed out, recalling especially her father's immediate approval of the younger man.

"I'm sure we'll all get along famously in the future, but I had planned on having you all to myself after I'd gotten rid of Irene and you'd finally seen the light! I most definitely did not anticipate having every room in the inn between yours and mine filled with relatives! I like to think I have a normal amount of courage but the thought of running that gauntlet every night was too much, even for me!"

"I'm amazed!" Savannah teased, thinking of Cord's obvious frustration over the past three days. "You let a little thing like a bunch of relatives hinder your male drives?"

"Little thing, my foot. Your father is nearly as large as I am and he looked in reasonably good shape in spite of the fact that he's got a number of years on me. Then there was the ever-present fear of sneaking into your room and finding your mother had dropped in for a cozy midnight chat with her darling daughter. And, of course, Aunt Ella had to suddenly take it into her head to become conscious of all the social niceties. She made it quite clear I'd better behave myself in front of my future in-laws if I wanted to keep their approval."

"Poor Cord," Savannah mocked laughingly.

"That's right, go ahead and make fun of me," he growled. "My wedding night has come at last and I intend to enjoy it thoroughly!"

Savannah felt the warmth flood her face at his

meaning and turned her head into his shoulder. "Cord! Someone will hear you!"

"The worst part about the past three days of enforced abstinence was that I knew exactly what I was missing!" He ignored Savannah's small squeak of embarrassed protest. She was becoming quite nervous at the thought of a neighboring couple on the dance floor overhearing. "Don't you have any compassion for me?" he pleaded morosely. "For the way I lay alone in my bed for the past two nights, staring at the ceiling and thinking of what it had been like having you in my bed? It never occurred to me that once I'd gotten you there I'd ever have to tolerate any more nights alone."

"It was probably very character-building," Savannah retorted spiritedly.

"It was very inspirational, I'll say that much for it," he noted grimly. "Why else do you think I managed to strong-arm that preacher into fitting us into his schedule this afternoon. He had planned a round of golf, you know. Do you have any idea how hard it is to talk a man out of his golf game? He was all set to put us off until tomorrow morning and I had to argue my case very forcefully."

Savannah giggled and decided she'd probably had too much champagne. Nestling snugly into his arms, she delighted in the possessive, tender hold Cord had on her. "My hero," she murmured with teasing admiration.

"Umm," he muttered, his voice lowering as he nuzzled the tip of her ear. "Your hero has just spent the most difficult three days of his life. I think it's time he had his reward, don't you?"

"You're tired of dancing already?" she inquired innocently.

"I'm tired of being driven slowly out of my mind by being able to hold you in my arms but not being able to make love to you. I've waited a long time for you, sweet amazon. . . ."

"Three whole days?" she chuckled, feeling her senses quicken at the seductive, gravelly tone of his voice.

"An entire lifetime," he corrected with soft passion. She could feel his warm breath stirring her hair. "Come be my wife, Savannah Harding!"

Savannah tipped her head back, suddenly and unaccountably experiencing a twinge of anxiety. For an instant she studied his face, read the barely restrained desire, the male hunger, and the passion there, and whispered in a tiny voice, "Oh, my darling, Cord! Are you very, very sure?"

The green eyes flamed gently with loving tenderness as he abruptly drew them both to a halt in the middle of the dance floor. Savannah was dimly aware that the music hadn't yet ceased and nearby couples were glancing toward the motionless pair. Heedless of the amused stares, Cord lifted his large hands to frame Savannah's still features.

"I have never been so sure of anything in my life, sweet Savannah. You are my one true love and from tonight forward I will never let you be parted from me. Do you believe me?"

Savannah stared up at the intent, rugged face,

curiously aware of an unexpected vulnerability in this hard man that she had never expected to find. It simultaneously thrilled her and made her feel incredibly protective. The love that welled within her was mirrored in her eyes for him to read.

"I believe you, Cord."

"Then come to me, my lovely wife, and let me show you my love in the one way a man like me must!"

Savannah said nothing but gave him a tremulous smile that seemed to provide its own answer. Cord's hands dropped from her face, and he put an arm around her and led her off the dance floor.

Cord's first act as her new husband that afternoon had been to have the management of the inn move Savannah's things from her room to his. He had been satisfied with that, but the management, apparently, had not. In addition to moving Savannah's suitcases, it had provided a chilled bottle of champagne picturesquely placed on the dressing table in a silver bucket. Two beribboned glasses stood on either side.

"How charming." Savannah smiled as Cord opened the door and she saw the inn's gift. She took a step forward to examine the label on the bottle, but Cord reached out to catch her hand and draw her back, even as he firmly shut and locked the door behind them.

"We'll drink it later," he told her with a purposeful urgency that Savannah knew she could not deny. Nor did she want to do so. She wondered if she would ever be able to deny this man anything when he looked at her with such love and need. With fingers that trembled ever so slightly she touched the side of his face and nodded her agreement.

"Later," she repeated.

He caught her hand and folded it against his chest, kissing it warmly before drawing her completely into his arms. "I need you far more than I need champagne right now," he half smiled, bending to cover her mouth in a languid, deeply arousing kiss that began to ignite the flame of desire Savannah experienced only around this man.

"I love you, Cord," she whispered, her eyes pools of liquid gold.

"For always?" he clarified in a husky voice.

"For always."

Without a word his hands went to the zipper of her long dress, and Savannah was both surprised and strangely touched to feel the trembling in his fingers. She wasn't the only one whose emotions were keyed to an almost painful pitch tonight!

"Ah, Savannah," he breathed as the dress dropped into a silky heap at her feet. "You are so perfect for me! Touch me, darling, undress me and let me feel your hands on my body. I've wanted you so badly. . . ."

It took an amazing amount of effort for Savannah to undue the buttons of Cord's shirt. Her pulse was racing so fast that she seemed to have lost control of her fingertips. But at last she was pushing the material off his shoulders, baring his hair-roughed chest to her touch. In another moment she felt her scrap of a bra falling away and Cord gently palming the nipple of one breast, his eyes meeting and holding hers.

Savannah sucked in her breath with a tiny betraying sound. Under his hand the pink tip hardened with desire, and Cord smiled with such male pleasure that Savannah knew exactly what he was thinking.

"Yes," he breathed, his words a thick, richly textured sound that ruffled all her nerve endings delightfully. "You're my woman at last. And I'm your man." He leaned forward, cupping the opposite breast in his hand and tonguing the nipple until it, too, responded. Savannah heard him groan softly before he straightened and suddenly swung her high into his arms.

Savannah's nails dug gently into the muscles of his shoulder as he carried her across the room and lowered her carefully to the turned-down bed. After slipping hurriedly out of the remainder of his clothes, he joined her there.

"I love you, I want you, and I need you, my sweet, sweet, Savannah," he growled hoarsely, one hand stroking the length of her smooth body, following the full contours of hip and thigh with clear possession and wonder. Every fiber in Savannah's strong female frame vibrated to his touch. There was an overpowering urge to please and trust and hold and love this one man who gloried in, rather than fled from, her own strength. A man who could match her passion and will. A true mate. Dreamily she slipped her arms around his neck, drawing him down to her.

"Oh, my love," he murmured, letting the full impact of his not-inconsiderable weight bear down on her until she was thoroughly trapped beneath him. "Tell me that you belong to me, that you'll never leave me!" he begged in a rasping voice.

"There could never be any doubt in my mind from now on, darling," she vowed. "You are mine and I am yours."

He curved his bare feet around her ankles and anchored her more firmly beneath him as his mouth began a sensuous trail of fire down her throat to her breast. Savannah began to stir almost unconsciously, responding to the building tension. Her hands stroked the sleekness of his back down to the lean waist and narrow hips, taking pleasure in the very feel of him.

"So strong and womanly and capable of such passion," he whispered, as his fingers found the protected area of her thighs and began to trace an erotic, thrilling pattern that soon had her twisting in need beneath him.

Her own hands seemed to have a will of their own, seeking, exploring, and touching. She heard his indrawn breath as he responded fully to her efforts.

"You make me lose my head, little amazon," he accused lovingly, turning onto his back and pulling her effortlessly onto his chest. Her hair spilled across his shoulder, and she heard herself whisper something warm and inviting that seemed to arouse him more than she would have thought possible.

Savannah found herself delighting in the new position, using it to explore him further, discovering what he responded to most, reveling in the sense of loving power she was experiencing. He seemed content to let the wave of her female passion flow over him, letting her take the lead until Savannah was riding such a crest of excitement and power, she thought she would burst. He smiled up at her, green eyes gleaming with humor and heat and pleasure.

"An amazon in my bed," he marveled, his hands circling her waist and sliding up her rib cage.

"Yes," she agreed, her mouth curving in a warm, laughing smile that made it clear how much she was enjoying herself. "Any objections?"

"None whatsoever," he assured her immediately, his grin of response holding just a hint of something savage and primitive. "Every man should be so lucky!"

Goaded by his laughing response and encouragement, Savannah lost herself even more thoroughly in her lovemaking, amazed at the newly revealed primitive side of her nature. Never in a million years would she have guessed herself to be capable of this degree of passion. Her strength flowed around her, encompassing him and binding him to her with ancient sorcery. This was her man and she would chain him to her with every bond she could forge.

Her own breath coming in little pants now, Savannah prepared to initiate the culmination of their lovemaking, the sense of control and mastery filling her with a desire to conclude her conquering of Cordell Harding.

And then, just as she shifted to take final command of the potent forces she had wrought, the room swung dizzily around her. Confused, she realized

Cord's hands had taken a firm grip on her waist and she was being swung off of him, back down onto the bed. She blinked, startled at the change of position, but before she could cry out her protest, he was looming over her, a giant, tenderly powerful male intent on claiming his woman.

"Cord!" she gasped, realizing he had reached some critical point in his need for her and was intent on satisfying it fully at last.

"I will take all of your strength now," he grated, parting her legs fiercely and letting her know his desire in the clearest possible terms.

"And I will take all of yours!" she vowed, wrapping her arms around his neck as he lowered himself against her.

"Yes!" he agreed and then coherent conversation became impossible as the room echoed to Savannah's soft feminine sounds and Cord's husky masculine cries.

A powerful rhythm was established between them that seemed to allow for the easy exchange of strength, love, and need. It grew in intensity and dynamics until Savannah was aware of nothing else in the universe except her man and the necessity of holding him to her with every ounce of her energy.

She was being held just as tightly. More so, in fact, because she could not make a move that did not respond to Cord's touch and driving need. He was making no secret of his possession. He was tuning her body in such a way that Savannah knew instinctively it would quicken only to his touch, his looks, his desires. He was mastering her, making her his for all time.

At last, with a final surge of controlled force, Savannah felt herself burst and dissolve into a shimmering, cascading display of fireworks. Dimly she heard his gasp of unrestrained satisfaction, and then, together, they collapsed damply into a motionless tangle of arms and legs.

It was a very long time before Savannah opened her eyes to find Cord's green gaze moving languidly over her. When he realized she was looking at him at last, he smiled down at her from his propped position.

"Hello, Mrs. Harding," he whispered, his fingers toying with a tangled lock of her hair. "Have I told you how glad I am that you love me?"

"You have no doubts on that issue?" She chuckled, reaching out to stroke his chest with gentle, caressing fingers.

"None whatsoever," he told her. "None at all. Do you have any doubts about me?"

"No," she whispered honestly.

"So much for the wonders of body-language communication." He grinned tenderly then he sobered. "My God!" he breathed passionately. "I don't know how I ever got along without you!"

Savannah laughed softly. "I didn't know what I'd been missing until I met you, either," she admitted.

He leaned back against the pillow, cradling her against him. Together they rested in silence for a few moments, regaining their energies and enjoying the quiet aftermath of their love.

"This may be a fitting time to open that champagne," Cord observed at last.

"Can I interest you in a bit of champagne in bed, sweetheart?"

"It sounds rather risqué," Savannah murmured doubtfully, tawny eyes laughing.

"Do you think so?" he asked doubtfully, turning his head to glance with narrowed eyes at the unoffending bottle on the dresser. "You could be right, but how can we be certain without trying it?"

"Good point," she agreed, yawning blissfully and edging aside slightly so that he could sit up. "I suppose only experimentation will reveal the truth."

"We may be risking hopeless corruption," Cord noted, getting to his feet and walking in unabashed nakedness across the room. He disappeared briefly into the bath, where Savannah heard water running in the sink. A moment later he reappeared, bearing a towel.

She watched in amusement and lazy happiness as he expertly uncorked the champagne, using the towel to control the foaming stuff.

"To my wife," he whispered, bearing the full glasses carefully back to bed and sitting down precariously.

"To my husband," Savannah returned, accepting her drink and sipping lightly.

"And to the wager that made it all possible," Cord intoned, taking another sip from his glass.

"I'm not sure I should drink to that," Savannah smiled humorously. "After all, you *did* cheat! And then had the nerve to act affronted when I accused you of it at the card table!" she added, chuckling.

"Sweetheart"—he smiled with intimate, warm menace—"I would have done whatever I had to do to get you. What's a man's honor at cards when something as important as claiming his woman is at stake?" He drained his glass and set it on the nightstand by the bed. "Remember in the future that I'll sink to just about any level when it comes to holding on to you!"

"Threats?" she teased lightly, glancing up at him from under her lashes.

"Now, whatever gave you that idea?" he inquired, one red brow lifting queryingly as he stretched out a hand to remove the glass from her fingers.

"Something about the way you looked at me this afternoon when you put this ring on my finger, I imagine," she confessed.

He lifted the hand bearing the ring in question and kissed the gold circlet. "Did it show?" he asked ruefully.

"The fact that you looked as if you'd just taken out the first payment on a gambling debt? Yes, I'm afraid it did. And don't look so falsely repentant! I know you too well now to be fooled by that expression," she commanded laughingly.

"Which brings up the little matter of the weekend you still owe me," he retorted leeringly.

"What weekend? You've had two nights with me! Surely that wipes out the wager!" Savannah protested with a grin, edging backward across the tangle of sheets at the look in his green eyes.

"The wager was for a weekend," he reminded her. "Not just any two nights. Then there's that scratch on the car. I intended collecting for that tonight, if you'll recall. . . ." With a lightning swift movement one large hand struck, grabbing Savannah's retreating ankle and yanking her gently flat on the bed. A moment later he was sprawled on top of her, wedging her as she squirmed and giggled firmly between himself and the bed.

"No fair," she squeaked as he anchored her wrists and used his heavy legs to trap her gently. "You can't use the excuse of those fictitious debts of mine every time you feel like making love to me!"

"You're sure of that?" he asked darkly, his fingers already making inroads into the most sensitive parts of her body.

"Yes!" she shot back, beginning to shiver deliciously at his touch.

"Want to bet?" he asked and then his mouth took hers, driving all thoughts of trying to renege on her debts out of Savannah's mind.

LOOK FOR NEXT MONTH'S
CANDLELIGHT ECSTASY ROMANCES: